The Patriot's Shadow

Olympus Reborn, Volume 1

Nandakishore and Tharun Vigneswar

Published by Draft2Digital, 2024.

THE PATRIOT'S SHADOW

First edition. November 12, 2024.

Copyright © 2024 Nandakishore and Tharun Vigneswar.

ISBN: 979-8230066798

Written by Nandakishore and Tharun Vigneswar.

Table of Contents

Chapter 1 | The Assignment....................1

Chapter 2 | Arrival at the Base....................7

Chapter 3 | First Steps 14

Chapter 4 | The Suspects....................22

Chapter 5 | A Hidden Agenda....................29

Chapter 6 | Shadows in the Night 35

Chapter 7 | The Deepening Web....................43

Chapter 8 | The Edge of War....................50

Chapter 9 | The War Within....................56

Chapter 10 | Into the Fire 62

Chapter 11 | The Heart of Olympus 68

Chapter 12 | The Final Countdown 75

Chapter 13 | The Dawn of Freedom....................81

Chapter 14 | The Last Stand....................87

Chapter 1
The Assignment

The rain poured down in sheets as Agent Jack Hayes navigated his way through the dark, empty streets leading to Langley. His headlights cut through the early morning mist, illuminating the sleek, nondescript entrance of the CIA's headquarters. The message from his handler had come at 3:00 a.m., summoning him to headquarters immediately. It was rare to be called in before dawn, and rarer still for the tone of the message—urgent, clipped, and cryptic.

Jack's instincts were already on high alert as he stepped out of his car, buttoning his rain-drenched coat. He glanced around as he entered the building, noting the guards at the front gate who gave him a silent nod, their faces as stern and unsmiling as always.

As he strode through the sprawling corridors of the CIA building, a sense of déjà vu washed over him. He'd spent countless hours here in briefings, debriefings, and high-stakes assignments that had taken him from the mountains of Afghanistan to the dense jungles of South America. But today felt different. Something was off.

At the end of the hall, he arrived at a secure elevator that led to a sub-basement briefing room, accessible only to a handful of agents. The door slid open silently, and he stepped inside, catching his reflection in the mirrored walls—a sharp, weathered face with piercing gray eyes, and a build that spoke of military precision honed over years. Jack didn't look like a stereotypical intelligence agent; he was more the kind of man you'd expect to find on the frontlines. And that was exactly how he liked it.

The elevator descended, and as the doors opened, Jack saw his handler, Director Tom Braddock, waiting in the dimly lit hallway. Braddock was in his fifties, with graying hair and a perpetually tired expression. His eyes, however, were sharp as steel, and he waved Jack into the room without a word. They entered the briefing room, and the door closed behind them with a hiss.

"Sit down, Hayes," Braddock said, gesturing toward a chair. His voice was low, gravelly, as if he hadn't slept in days.

Jack took a seat, watching Braddock as he settled into the chair across from him. A large digital screen flickered to life on the wall, displaying a map of Eastern Europe with a red dot pulsing ominously near the border of Romania and Ukraine.

"Do you know about Project Olympus?" Braddock asked, studying Jack's expression.

Jack shook his head. "Heard whispers, but nothing concrete. Experimental weapon, right?"

Braddock's gaze remained fixed on Jack. "More than experimental. It's a fully autonomous stealth drone, capable of infiltrating any enemy defense system and launching strikes with surgical precision. Untraceable. Indestructible."

Jack let that sink in. "And it's gone missing?"

"Not exactly. Two days ago, a transport convoy in Romania carrying critical components for Olympus was ambushed. The convoy's security detail—Navy SEALs, trained operators—was eliminated. No survivors. The components, and the encrypted design specs, are now in the wind."

Braddock clicked a button on the console in front of him, and an image appeared on the screen—a burned-out convoy, the charred remains of vehicles twisted and unrecognizable. Scattered around the wreckage were black body bags, the remains of men who'd once been America's elite.

"Intel points to a new player," Braddock continued. "A private group called the Iron Hand, led by an ex-Russian major named Ivan Volkov. Operates in the shadows, funds insurgencies, sabotages governments. And now, they're after Olympus. We believe they plan to sell it on the black market."

Jack's eyes narrowed. "And you're sending me in to retrieve it."

Braddock leaned forward. "This isn't just a retrieval mission, Jack. We need you to identify how the ambush was coordinated. Someone on the inside knew the exact route, time, and strength of that convoy. You're being sent to root out a traitor."

Silence hung heavy in the room as Jack absorbed the weight of the assignment. A covert mission to infiltrate a U.S. military base in Eastern Europe, uncover a mole, and recover a weapon powerful enough to change the course of any battle.

"When do I leave?" Jack asked, his tone steady.

"Tonight. Your cover will be that of a liaison officer, sent to assist in security assessments on behalf of the Pentagon. General Curtis Briggs, the base commander, has been briefed to expect you, though he wasn't thrilled about the idea. He's ex-Delta Force—doesn't take kindly to CIA oversight."

Jack smirked. "I'll try not to step on any toes."

Braddock sighed, his gaze softening for a brief moment. "Jack...this one's different. The stakes are high, and we don't know how deep the leak goes. Trust no one."

The warning was clear. Jack nodded, rising from his seat as Braddock handed him a secure phone, a forged military ID, and a dossier with more details on the key personnel stationed at the base.

Jack's thoughts raced as he boarded the military transport bound for Eastern Europe. His mission dossier lay open on his lap, pages filled with profiles, security clearance codes, and intel on his potential allies—and enemies.

Captain Sarah Keller—an Army intelligence officer. Reputation for being brilliant but headstrong. Rumored to be frustrated with the limitations placed on her investigation into the ambush.

Sergeant Ben "Buzz" Thompson—one of the few survivors of the transport's security detail, currently in critical condition at a nearby hospital. His last communication hinted at "insider eyes" watching their movements.

Dr. Emma Reyes—a civilian engineer and Project Olympus' lead scientist, with clearance levels beyond most officers at the base. Despite her crucial role, she was known to be critical of military intervention. Her reluctance to work on Olympus raised questions.

The hours passed in tense silence as the transport soared over the Atlantic. Jack reviewed the files again and again, committing details to memory, considering each angle, each personality. It felt like he was playing a game of chess with invisible opponents, trying to anticipate their moves before they even considered them.

As the transport touched down on the rain-soaked tarmac of the military base, Jack felt the familiar surge of adrenaline that came with stepping into hostile territory. Even in friendly territory, he knew he could trust no one.

The sprawling base was a fortress—high walls, armed guards, watchtowers illuminated against the stormy night sky. The air smelled of wet concrete and diesel, the distant hum of machines filling the cold, damp air. Jack disembarked, greeted by two soldiers who led him to an armored vehicle that would take him to the base's command center.

As the vehicle rumbled across the compound, he caught glimpses of soldiers going through nighttime drills, their silhouettes stark against the floodlights. The base was as active as any he'd seen, but there was a tension in the air—a sense of unease that lingered in every glance, every movement.

The armored vehicle stopped outside the main command building, a bunker-like structure lined with reinforced concrete and barbed wire. As he stepped out, Jack was greeted by the stern gaze of General Curtis Briggs, a broad-shouldered man with a square jaw and steely eyes that seemed to assess every detail of Jack in an instant.

"Agent Hayes, I presume," Briggs said, his voice a low rumble.

Jack nodded, keeping his tone neutral. "General Briggs. Thank you for accommodating me."

Briggs didn't bother to hide his skepticism. "I'm not one to mince words, Hayes. I don't like this. My men are disciplined and loyal. I don't need the CIA coming in and stirring up suspicion."

"With respect, General," Jack replied, "my presence here isn't to question your men's loyalty. It's to make sure Project Olympus doesn't end up in enemy hands."

Briggs's jaw tightened, but he gave a curt nod. "Follow me. Captain Keller's waiting in the briefing room. She'll bring you up to speed."

They walked in silence through the command center's narrow, dimly lit halls. Jack could feel the eyes of soldiers and officers following him, their faces a mix of curiosity and suspicion. News of the ambush had undoubtedly shaken them, and his presence could only add to the tension.

Finally, they reached the briefing room, where Captain Sarah Keller stood waiting. She was tall, with dark hair pulled back in a tight bun, and a sharp, analytical gaze. Her posture was rigid, her expression unreadable as she extended a hand.

"Agent Hayes," she said crisply, her handshake firm. "I've been expecting you."

Jack noted the hint of irritation in her voice, though she hid it well. "Captain Keller," he replied. "I'm looking forward to working together."

Keller's gaze flicked to General Briggs, then back to Jack. "Let's get one thing clear," she said, her tone direct. "I don't like being kept in the dark about my own mission. If you have information about the ambush, I expect full transparency."

Jack's lips quirked into a half-smile.

Chapter 2
Arrival at the Base

The transport helicopter descended into the fog-laden valley as the faint outline of Outpost Grey appeared through the mist. The base was nestled against steep cliffs, with high walls topped with razor wire and guard towers perched at strategic points. Jack Hayes sat inside, his face expressionless, absorbing every detail as they approached. The icy wind seeped through the cabin, carrying the smell of diesel and damp earth. He adjusted his coat, his mind already calculating the challenges of the terrain and the isolated layout of the facility.

As the helicopter touched down on the landing pad, Jack disembarked, his boots sinking into the wet gravel. He took a deep breath, his senses immediately picking up the faint, metallic scent of gunpowder in the cold morning air. A distant rumble of machinery echoed from somewhere within the compound. Soldiers moved with purpose, some on patrol, others drilling near the barracks. Their faces were hardened, their expressions guarded.

Jack didn't have to be told that Outpost Grey was tense. The ambush and loss of Olympus technology had rocked the base, and whispers of suspicion had likely spread. His presence, a CIA operative with a vague "liaison" cover, would only fuel the speculation. The base was on edge, and that suited him just fine.

He worked best in places where people were already watching over their shoulders.

Waiting for him at the edge of the landing pad was Captain Sarah Keller, standing stiffly in her combat fatigues. She looked even more severe in the daylight—tall, with dark hair pulled tightly into a bun, her eyes narrowed against the mist. Her gaze held a touch of annoyance, the same look she'd given him in their initial introduction back in the command center.

She gave him a curt nod. "Agent Hayes. We have a lot to go over."

Jack returned the nod, taking a moment to assess her. Keller had a reputation for being tough, brilliant, and exacting, but he could tell that recent events had unsettled her. He could see the subtle tension in her jaw, the way her fingers twitched at her side. She was operating on high alert, and he would have to tread carefully with her.

"Lead the way, Captain," he said.

They walked across the compound in silence, passing clusters of soldiers who eyed Jack with a mix of curiosity and suspicion. The outpost's buildings were utilitarian—gray and unadorned, designed more for function than comfort. To the left was a sprawling hangar filled with military vehicles and supply crates, some marked with heavy red "CLASSIFIED" labels. Beyond it lay the barracks, and further still, a section of fenced-off land with watchtowers, guarded as if it held the base's most critical assets.

As they walked, Keller began her briefing, her voice clipped and precise.

"Outpost Grey was established as a forward operating base for monitoring and intercepting hostile activity along the

Eastern European borders. We handle everything from surveillance to tactical operations, with personnel from various branches." She paused, giving him a sideways glance. "Until now, our operations have been smooth, secure. The ambush changed that."

Jack kept his expression neutral. "I read the initial report on the convoy. SEAL team eliminated, components stolen. How did the intel on the convoy route get compromised?"

Keller's jaw tightened. "We don't know. The convoy route was highly classified, known only to select personnel. Whoever orchestrated the ambush knew exactly where they'd be and when. This was no random attack."

As they reached the main command building, Jack glanced up at the rows of cameras lining the roof, all tracking their movements with cold, unblinking eyes. Security was airtight. Whoever had infiltrated the convoy's plans had access to some of the base's most secure information.

Inside, Keller led him down a corridor lined with steel doors and thick, reinforced glass. The sound of her boots echoed off the walls as they approached the entrance to a secure briefing room, guarded by two armed Marines. They saluted Keller, giving Jack a quick once-over before stepping aside.

The briefing room was dimly lit, with walls lined in dark panels. A large digital screen dominated the far wall, displaying a topographical map of the region. Waiting inside was General Curtis Briggs, standing with his arms crossed. His granite-like expression remained unchanged as he watched them enter.

"Agent Hayes," he greeted, his voice a gravelly rumble. "Glad you made it. I trust Captain Keller has given you the basics?"

Jack nodded, taking a seat across from the general. "I've been briefed on the ambush and the mission parameters. I'll be working closely with Captain Keller to investigate the breach."

Briggs gave Keller a brief nod, signaling her to begin the more detailed debriefing. She stepped forward, clicking a remote in her hand, and a new map flashed up on the screen, showing the ambush site in high resolution.

"The convoy was en route from a classified research facility in Romania, transporting three critical components for Project Olympus," Keller explained, her tone sharp and focused. "The attackers were waiting in this valley"—she pointed at the map—"where visibility was limited, and the terrain favored an ambush. We believe there were two teams: one handling explosives and heavy weaponry, the other performing the extraction."

She clicked again, and satellite images of the wrecked vehicles and bodies appeared. The level of destruction was brutal, efficient. Jack noted the pattern of debris, the precision in the targeting. Whoever had done this wasn't just skilled—they were professionals.

"What about survivors?" he asked, his eyes narrowing at the image.

Keller hesitated. "One. Sergeant Ben Thompson. He was found unconscious near the wreckage with severe injuries. He's currently in critical condition at the base infirmary and hasn't been able to give a full account of what happened. But he managed to send one last communication before he blacked out."

She pressed another button, and an audio recording played over the speakers, crackling with static. Thompson's voice, weak and strained, came through, barely audible.

"...ambush... they knew... we were coming... eyes... on the inside..."

The recording ended, leaving a heavy silence in its wake. Jack felt a chill run through him. "Eyes on the inside" meant someone on the base had provided intel to the enemy.

Keller glanced at Briggs, her lips pressing into a thin line. "It's possible that someone within our own ranks tipped off the attackers."

Briggs's expression hardened, his face a mask of anger barely contained. "You're here to root out that traitor, Hayes. I don't care how long it takes or how deep this goes. This base operates on loyalty and discipline. We don't tolerate traitors."

Jack nodded, though he knew it wouldn't be that simple. Traitors rarely announced themselves; they hid behind layers of loyalty and silence. The trick would be identifying who, among these hardened soldiers, had cracked.

Briggs turned his attention back to Keller. "Captain, bring Hayes up to speed on the base personnel and all activities connected to Project Olympus. I want him fully briefed on everyone who might have had access to that convoy's route."

Keller nodded, signaling Jack to follow her out of the briefing room. They walked in silence, her gaze focused straight ahead, her expression unreadable. Once they reached her office, a small room cluttered with files, maps, and a series of monitors displaying live feeds from various parts of the base, she gestured for him to sit.

She handed him a file, thick and heavy with documents. "This contains the personnel files of everyone with access to Project Olympus intel, as well as those involved in the convoy route planning. You'll find names, backgrounds, psych evaluations... everything."

Jack opened the file and began skimming through it. Names and faces flashed by—men and women who'd dedicated their lives to the military, each with their own histories, accomplishments, and, potentially, secrets.

"I've done a preliminary assessment," Keller continued, leaning against the edge of her desk. "But as you can imagine, these are my colleagues. I have to tread carefully."

Jack gave a small nod. "Understood. I'll handle the questioning myself. But I'll need access to everything related to Olympus—lab reports, test data, even communications logs."

Keller hesitated. "That's... a lot of classified information."

He met her gaze. "If there's a mole in your ranks, I need a full picture of their activities and communications."

She sighed but nodded. "Fine. I'll grant you access, but only under supervision. General Briggs isn't exactly thrilled about the idea of a CIA agent combing through our records."

"Neither am I," Jack replied dryly. "But it's the job."

They locked eyes for a moment, a mutual understanding passing between them. There was a professional respect there, but also an unspoken wariness. They both knew they were dealing with something bigger than either of them, and trust would have to be earned, not assumed.

Jack spent the next several hours familiarizing himself with the personnel files. He studied photos, examined commendations, and noted any red flags or discrepancies in backgrounds. He highlighted a few individuals whose behavior or associations seemed out of place, but it was too early to draw any conclusions.

After going through the files, he moved to his temporary quarters—a stark, windowless room equipped with only the essentials.

Chapter 3
First Steps

The next morning, Jack awoke to the sound of rain drumming against the metal roof of his quarters. The dim light filtering through the base cast long shadows, as if Outpost Grey itself had secrets to keep. He dressed quickly, slipping on his coat and securing his ID badge. Today, he would dive deeper into the events surrounding the ambush, starting with a visit to the site of the attack.

Outside, the rain had turned the compound's gravel paths into slippery sludge. Soldiers moved about, their heads down, faces turned away from the cold. There was a quiet determination to their movements, but also a tension simmering beneath the surface. The atmosphere was heavy, a mixture of distrust and fear.

Jack made his way across the compound toward the garage, where a convoy vehicle was waiting for him. Captain Keller stood beside it, wrapped in a dark green field jacket, her face set in a hard, unreadable expression. Her jaw was clenched as she looked out into the rain, lost in thought.

"Agent Hayes," she said, nodding as he approached. "We'll be heading out to the ambush site. It's a bit of a drive, but it'll give you a chance to see the terrain."

"Good," Jack replied. "The more I understand the area, the better."

Keller climbed into the driver's seat, and Jack took the passenger side. As she started the engine, he could sense her unease—though whether it was about the mission or him, he wasn't entirely sure. The vehicle rumbled to life, and they pulled out of the base, the thick fog swallowing them as they drove down the winding, muddy road.

They drove in silence for the first few miles, the dense forest pressing in on either side of the narrow road. Jack studied the trees, the dense underbrush, and the sheer cliffs looming above. It was an ideal location for an ambush—isolated, with plenty of places to hide and limited escape routes.

As they rounded a curve, Keller finally spoke, her voice low and steady. "I've been stationed here for three years, and I've never seen an operation as meticulously planned as this ambush. Whoever did this... they knew exactly what they were doing. They exploited every weakness in the convoy's route."

Jack turned to look at her, his gaze thoughtful. "And you're sure no one on the base knew about the route details outside of your team?"

She shook her head. "Positive. Only a handful of people had access to that intel—myself, General Briggs, the logistics team, and a few others. Security was tight."

"Then we're dealing with someone who has intimate knowledge of our procedures—and access to classified information," Jack said, his voice thoughtful.

Keller clenched her jaw, her hands gripping the wheel tighter. "That's what bothers me the most. I know my team. I trust them. But... someone on the inside had to be involved."

Jack watched her for a moment, considering her words. Trust was a fragile thing, especially in the intelligence world. He had learned long ago that the people closest to you could also be the most dangerous.

After nearly an hour, they reached the ambush site—a narrow valley surrounded by steep, jagged cliffs. The remnants of burned-out vehicles and scattered debris lay strewn across the muddy ground, a grim reminder of the deadly encounter. The smell of charred metal and gasoline still lingered in the air, mixing with the damp, earthy scent of the forest.

Keller parked the vehicle and they stepped out, each taking in the scene in silence. The destruction was stark, brutal. Jack felt a chill run down his spine as he surveyed the blackened wreckage, imagining the chaos and violence that had unfolded here just days before.

"This was the lead vehicle," Keller said, pointing to a twisted mass of metal that had once been an armored transport. "It took the brunt of the attack. The ambushers used RPGs to disable the convoy, then moved in with automatic weapons."

Jack knelt beside the wreckage, running his fingers over the charred metal. "Looks like they knew exactly where to hit. The explosion would have forced the other vehicles to stop, making them easy targets."

Keller nodded. "Exactly. They boxed them in, trapped them."

Jack stood, scanning the surrounding cliffs. "Do we know how many attackers there were?"

"We estimate at least fifteen, based on the shell casings and tracks we found. But we have no leads on who they were or where they came from." Keller hesitated, glancing around the site. "The only clue we have is the message Sergeant Thompson managed to send before he lost consciousness—'eyes on the inside.'"

Jack considered this, his mind racing. "Then the traitor didn't just provide intel—they coordinated with the attackers in real-time."

Keller's face darkened. "Which means they could still be on the base, watching our every move."

As Jack continued to examine the scene, he noticed a glint of metal half-buried in the mud near one of the destroyed vehicles. He knelt down, brushing the dirt away to reveal a small, twisted piece of equipment—a broken communication device, burned but still partially intact.

"What's this?" he murmured, holding it up for Keller to see.

Her eyes widened. "That's not standard issue. I've never seen a device like that before."

Jack examined it closely. The device was small, designed for covert use, and bore no identifying marks. But there was something unsettlingly familiar about its design, as if it had been created specifically for clandestine operations.

"I'll need to take this back to the base for analysis," he said, slipping it into his pocket. "Maybe our tech team can pull something from it—an ID number, a frequency, anything."

Keller nodded, though her expression remained tense. "If that device belonged to the attackers, then they were using tech we haven't seen before. This was no ordinary ambush, Agent Hayes. These people... they're professionals."

Jack's mind raced as he followed her back to the vehicle, his thoughts a whirlwind of theories and questions. The device was sophisticated, possibly military-grade, and its presence only deepened the mystery surrounding the ambush. Who were these attackers? And why were they so determined to acquire Olympus?

Back at the base, Jack's first stop was the infirmary, where Sergeant Ben Thompson lay in critical condition. The survivor's room was small and sterile, with monitors beeping softly in the background. Thompson lay on the bed, hooked up to various machines, his face pale and gaunt.

Jack stepped inside quietly, nodding to the nurse before approaching the bed. Thompson's eyes were closed, his breathing shallow and labored. The nurse leaned in, whispering, "He's been in and out of consciousness. But you might get a few words out of him."

Jack nodded, pulling a chair close to the bed. He leaned forward, his voice low. "Sergeant Thompson... can you hear me?"

The man's eyelids fluttered, and he opened his eyes, his gaze hazy and unfocused. It took a moment, but recognition flickered in his expression as he looked at Jack.

"Agent Hayes?" he rasped, his voice barely audible.

Jack nodded, leaning closer. "I need to know what happened out there, Sergeant. You sent a message—'eyes on the inside.' Do you remember?"

Thompson's eyes flickered with fear, and he swallowed, his voice a faint whisper. "They... they knew everything. Every detail. We didn't stand a chance."

"Who knew, Sergeant? Who betrayed you?" Jack asked, keeping his tone steady but urgent.

Thompson's gaze grew distant, as if he were reliving the ambush in his mind. "We... trusted them. Thought they were... one of us. But... they turned on us."

"Who?" Jack pressed, his heart pounding.

Thompson's eyes closed, his breathing shallow and ragged. "Couldn't see... but... he was watching. Always watching..."

The heart monitor beeped faster as Thompson's body tensed, his face contorted in pain. A nurse rushed over, adjusting his IV, and Jack stepped back, watching helplessly as Thompson slipped back into unconsciousness.

The nurse glanced at Jack, her expression apologetic. "I'm sorry, Agent Hayes. That's all he can manage for now."

Jack nodded, frustration gnawing at him. Thompson had been their best hope for identifying the traitor, and now they were back to square one. He would have to rely on his own instincts and observations—and the evidence they'd gathered so far.

As he left the infirmary, Jack's mind churned with the implications of Thompson's words. Someone on the base—a person they trusted—had orchestrated the attack, feeding information to the enemy with deadly precision.

Determined to find answers, Jack headed to the tech lab to have the mysterious communication device analyzed. The lab was a sterile, high-tech space filled with computers, monitors, and specialized equipment. A team of technicians worked in silence, their eyes glued to screens displaying streams of data.

Jack stared at the small device in his hand as he entered the tech lab. Dr. Samir Patel, the lead technician, was already at his station, surrounded by multiple screens and equipment humming quietly in the background. The lab smelled faintly of metal and disinfectant, a sterile environment where secrets were often uncovered.

"Dr. Patel, I need you to take a look at something," Jack said, holding out the communication device.

Patel adjusted his glasses, taking the device from Jack's hand with a look of curiosity. "What do we have here?" he muttered, turning the device over in his hands. "This is definitely not standard issue."

Jack leaned against the desk, watching intently as Patel began examining the small, twisted piece of equipment under a microscope. "What makes it so different?" Jack asked, his voice low but focused.

"This isn't something we've ever seen before," Patel said, his tone thoughtful. "It's advanced, no doubt about it. This kind of tech... it looks like something designed for covert ops. Whoever used this didn't want to be detected."

Jack's mind raced as Patel connected the device to one of the lab's primary systems. The technician's fingers moved swiftly over the keyboard, bringing up a series of readouts. "Let's see what we can find."

The silence between them was tense as the data slowly began to populate on the screen. Jack could feel his pulse quicken with each passing second. The room felt heavy with anticipation, the answers they were looking for potentially lying in this unassuming piece of broken equipment.

Finally, Patel straightened, his fingers still hovering over the keyboard. "I think I've got something," he said, pulling up a series of encrypted files. "There's a communication log here. Someone was using this device to transmit and receive signals. But the data is heavily encrypted."

Jack's brow furrowed. "Is there any way to decrypt it?"

Patel gave him a look of hesitation. "It will take some time. We'll need access to higher-level decryption tools, and even then, it could take hours... maybe longer."

Jack's impatience was evident, but he knew the drill. He'd been in situations where the clock was ticking and information had to be extracted with precision. "Do what you can. Let me know as soon as you get anything useful."

Patel nodded, his focus returning to the screens. "Understood, Agent Hayes."

As Jack left the tech lab, he felt the weight of the case pressing down on him. The ambush had been meticulously planned, and someone on the inside had played a key role in the execution. Every lead seemed to circle back to the same troubling conclusion: there was a traitor among them, someone who had access to critical intel and was feeding it to the enemy.

Jack's thoughts drifted back to his interviews. He needed to dig deeper. The soldiers closest to the operation, those with direct access to the convoy's route—one of them had to know something. But who? And why did they do it?

He headed for the records room next, determined to get a better sense of the people involved. The room was small and cramped, filled with file boxes and storage units. It was a quiet, almost oppressive space, but Jack was used to it. The weight of the files and the weight of the truth they might hold were familiar companions.

Chapter 4
The Suspects

Back at Outpost Grey, Jack Hayes was deep in the records room, a small, dimly lit space tucked away near the command center. Shelves lined with file boxes and digital storage units loomed over him, each one holding information on the hundreds of personnel who had served at the base over the years. The walls were decorated with photographs of past commanding officers and group shots of soldiers, a silent reminder of the camaraderie and trust that Outpost Grey was built on.

But Jack knew that at least one of the faces among those hundreds belonged to a traitor.

Earlier that morning, he'd started his first round of interviews, focusing on those with access to Project Olympus intel and those connected to the convoy's logistics. His job was not only to ask questions but to listen, to observe the tiny shifts in body language, the hesitation in responses, the discomfort that might betray a hidden agenda.

With a list of names in hand, Jack was methodical. Each suspect represented a puzzle piece that might complete the bigger picture.

Interview 1: Lieutenant Daniel Mason

Jack's first meeting was with Lieutenant Daniel Mason, a logistics officer who had been part of the team planning the convoy route. Mason was a young, fit officer in his early thirties, with short blond hair and an easygoing smile. But when he stepped into Jack's makeshift interview room, his expression shifted from casual to tense. The weight of the investigation had clearly gotten to him.

"Lieutenant Mason," Jack greeted him, motioning to the chair across from him. Mason took a seat, his gaze darting around the room before finally settling on Jack.

"Agent Hayes," Mason replied, folding his hands tightly. "I, uh... wasn't expecting to be questioned."

"Not many people do," Jack said, his tone neutral. He placed Mason's personnel file on the table, flipping it open. "You're aware that the convoy route was compromised, resulting in the deaths of multiple soldiers. I'm here to find out who was responsible for that leak, Lieutenant."

Mason nodded, visibly swallowing. "I understand, sir. It's just... shocking, you know? We've always been a close team."

Jack watched him carefully, noting the strain in his voice. "You were responsible for coordinating the convoy logistics, correct? Including the route?"

"Yes, but everything I did was by the book," Mason insisted, leaning forward. "I'm as devastated as anyone about what happened. Some of those guys were my friends."

Jack nodded, letting a pause linger. "Tell me, Lieutenant, in the days leading up to the convoy, did you notice anything unusual? Any conversations that stood out? Changes in security protocols?"

Mason hesitated, his fingers tapping on the edge of the table. "Now that you mention it... I did see Captain Langston in the logistics office the day before the convoy left. He said he was checking up on the route, but that was unusual. He's usually hands-off with this kind of stuff."

"Captain Langston?" Jack asked, making a note in his notebook. "He had no direct involvement with Project Olympus, correct?"

Mason shook his head. "Not to my knowledge. But he seemed interested in the convoy for some reason. I didn't think much of it at the time."

Jack leaned back, studying Mason. He could sense the young officer was telling the truth, but he also knew how easy it was for small, seemingly insignificant details to slip by unnoticed.

"All right, Lieutenant," Jack said finally. "Thank you. If you remember anything else, contact me directly."

Mason stood up, visibly relieved, and nodded. "Of course, Agent Hayes. I'll do whatever I can to help."

As Mason left, Jack jotted down notes about Captain Langston. He'd need to follow up on this lead, even if it seemed thin. In his line of work, no detail was too small to investigate.

Interview 2: Captain Robert Langston

Later that afternoon, Jack arranged to meet with Captain Robert Langston. Langston was in his early forties, a rugged, broad-shouldered officer with years of combat experience and a no-nonsense demeanor. He walked into the room with the steady, confident stride of a man who'd faced down worse than a CIA interrogation.

"Captain Langston," Jack greeted him, gesturing to the chair. Langston nodded curtly and sat down, his piercing eyes locking onto Jack's with a mix of suspicion and defiance.

"I'll be direct, Agent Hayes," Langston said, crossing his arms. "I don't appreciate being dragged in here like I'm some kind of criminal."

Jack raised an eyebrow, unfazed by the captain's aggression. "I'm here to gather information, Captain. If you've done nothing wrong, you have nothing to worry about."

Langston grunted, his gaze hard. "Fine. Ask your questions."

Jack pulled out Langston's personnel file, taking a moment to scan it before he spoke. "You were seen in the logistics office the day before the convoy's departure. Can you explain why you were there?"

Langston's expression remained stony, but his eyes flickered briefly. "I had my reasons."

"Care to elaborate?" Jack pressed, his tone cool and unwavering.

Langston shifted, clearly uncomfortable. "Look, I've been suspicious of this whole Olympus project from the start. I don't like how much secrecy surrounds it. I was in the logistics office to see if there was anything unusual about the convoy route. I wanted to make sure everything was aboveboard."

Jack studied him, noting the slight tension in his jaw. "Did you find anything unusual?"

Langston hesitated, and for a moment, Jack thought he saw a flicker of fear in the captain's eyes. "No. Everything was normal, as far as I could tell."

Jack's gaze narrowed. Langston was hiding something. "Captain, if there's anything you're not telling me, now is the time. Lives have been lost, and more could be at risk."

Langston's jaw tightened, and he looked away, his expression hardening. "I've said all I have to say, Agent Hayes. If you want to accuse me of something, go ahead. Otherwise, I have a job to do."

Jack watched as Langston stood up, a wall of defiance in his posture. "This isn't over, Captain," he said quietly. "I'll be following up on this."

Langston didn't respond, simply giving Jack a final, icy glare before walking out of the room.

Interview 3: Specialist Lisa Monroe

Jack's final interview of the day was with Specialist Lisa Monroe, a quiet, unassuming woman with dark hair pulled back into a neat bun and a nervous expression. Monroe worked in communications and had been responsible for monitoring convoy channels on the day of the ambush. She seemed wary as she entered the room, her gaze darting nervously toward Jack before she took a seat.

"Specialist Monroe," Jack greeted her, keeping his tone calm. He could tell she was intimidated by the situation, and he didn't want to spook her.

"Agent Hayes," she replied softly, her voice barely above a whisper.

"You were on duty in communications during the convoy's departure. Is that correct?"

Monroe nodded quickly. "Yes, sir. I monitored their radio channels and kept an eye on the comms systems. Everything seemed normal when they left."

Jack leaned forward, watching her closely. "Did you notice any unusual activity on the channels? Anything out of the ordinary?"

Monroe hesitated, chewing her lip. "There... there was one strange thing," she admitted, her voice barely audible. "About an hour before the ambush, I picked up a brief transmission on an encrypted channel. It was just static at first, but then... there was a voice."

Jack's heart quickened. "What did the voice say?"

Monroe's hands trembled slightly as she recalled the moment. "It was just a few words. It said, 'They're ready. Proceed as planned.' Then the line went dead."

Jack's eyes narrowed. "Did you report this transmission to anyone?"

Monroe shook her head, looking ashamed. "No, sir. I thought... I thought it was nothing. Just some interference or a random transmission. But now, with everything that's happened, I think... I think it was them."

Jack felt a surge of frustration. This small oversight might have changed everything if she had reported it in time. But he kept his expression neutral. "Thank you, Specialist Monroe. If you remember anything else, let me know."

Monroe nodded, a haunted look in her eyes as she stood and quickly left the room.

As the evening wore on, Jack returned to his quarters, his mind racing with the new information. Each interview had revealed more pieces of the puzzle, but none of them seemed to fit perfectly. Lieutenant Mason's suspicions about Captain Langston were intriguing but inconclusive. Langston's evasiveness was suspicious, and his disdain for Project Olympus was noted, but Jack had no concrete evidence to tie him to the ambush. And Specialist Monroe's report of the encrypted transmission... that was the most troubling revelation yet.

Jack sat at his desk, poring over the notes he had taken. If there was a mole on the base, they were clever—someone skilled enough to evade detection while feeding information to the enemy in real-time.

But he still had no name, no clear lead. The tension was building, and Jack could feel the weight of the investigation pressing down on him. If he didn't find the traitor soon, more lives could be lost, and the conspiracy that had already started to unfold could spiral beyond their control.

Chapter 5
A Hidden Agenda

The next morning, Jack Hayes sat in Outpost Grey's cramped intel analysis room, surrounded by files, photographs, and stacks of papers. Diagrams and maps of the convoy's route covered one wall, with a red line tracing the doomed path they had taken. Each piece of information was tagged with sticky notes and red markers, showing potential links, suspicions, and theories in chaotic detail. The sight of it all would be overwhelming to most people, but for Jack, it was just the beginning.

The small communication device he'd discovered at the ambush site lay in the center of the desk, next to a folder labeled "Classified - Project Olympus". Jack had sent it to the tech team the previous evening, and their report had landed in his inbox early that morning. He'd spent the last hour reading their findings, each page revealing more than he'd hoped but also raising questions he hadn't anticipated.

The device was unlike anything standard-issue in the U.S. military. It was a sleek, covert communication tool, compact and built for encrypted transmissions. Its design hinted at something custom-made, perhaps crafted by a private manufacturer specializing in off-the-books tech. The tech team's analysis indicated that it had been modified to emit a minimal heat signature, making it nearly impossible to detect with standard radar or tracking equipment. In short, it was perfect for covert operations.

What's more, the device used a frequency that matched one registered to a private contractor—Paramount Defense, a shadowy defense firm known for operating in conflict zones but often shrouded in allegations of dubious dealings. Jack was familiar with Paramount Defense; he had crossed paths with them before. Their involvement in Project Olympus could only mean one thing: there were powerful, unseen forces at play here.

Jack sat back, running his hands through his hair as he processed the information. If Paramount Defense had a hand in this, it meant there was more at stake than just the stolen intel. The ambush might have been part of a far larger plan—a conspiracy that reached beyond Outpost Grey and into the halls of corporate and military power.

Determined to get answers, Jack left the analysis room and made his way to General Briggs' office. Briggs was the commanding officer of Outpost Grey and the highest-ranking official overseeing Project Olympus. Jack knew that if anyone could shed light on the true purpose of Olympus and its connections to Paramount Defense, it was Briggs.

Briggs' office was at the end of a long, narrow hallway, guarded by a pair of armed soldiers who eyed Jack suspiciously as he approached. He showed them his identification, and after a tense moment, they stepped aside, allowing him to enter.

Inside, the general sat behind a massive oak desk, papers neatly arranged before him. He looked up as Jack entered, his expression unreadable. Briggs was an imposing figure—tall and broad-shouldered, with graying hair and a face etched by years of experience. His cold, calculating eyes fixed on Jack with a mixture of curiosity and annoyance.

"Agent Hayes," Briggs said, his voice low and gravelly. "I trust you have a reason for barging in here unannounced."

Jack met his gaze, refusing to be intimidated. "I do, General. I need answers, and I believe you're the only one who can provide them."

Briggs raised an eyebrow, a faint smirk playing at the corners of his mouth. "Is that so? Go ahead, Agent. Ask your questions."

Jack took a seat across from Briggs, placing the report on Paramount Defense on the desk. "I want to know about Paramount Defense's involvement in Project Olympus. Their communication device was found at the ambush site, which suggests they've been monitoring us—or worse, collaborating with whoever planned the attack."

Briggs's expression hardened, and he glanced down at the report. "Paramount Defense is a contractor. They've provided logistical support for Olympus, but their involvement ends there. If their equipment was found at the site, it could have been stolen, planted, or acquired on the black market."

Jack shook his head. "That's a convenient excuse, General. But this device wasn't just any piece of equipment—it was customized, using a proprietary frequency registered to Paramount. That points to something more than simple logistical support."

Briggs remained silent, his eyes narrowing as he studied Jack. After a long pause, he finally spoke. "Olympus is a highly sensitive project, Agent Hayes. Even you are not fully cleared to know its scope. Suffice it to say, Olympus has attracted a variety of interests—some friendly, some not."

Jack leaned forward, his tone sharp. "The ambush wasn't just an attack, General. It was a surgical strike, executed with precise information that only an insider could have provided. I have soldiers telling me they saw unusual activity in the days leading up to the ambush—officers out of place, encrypted transmissions. And now, we have evidence linking this to a company notorious for operating in moral gray areas."

Briggs's gaze grew colder, his jaw tightening. "You're playing a dangerous game, Hayes. I suggest you tread carefully."

Jack's eyes narrowed. "I'm not here to play games, General. I'm here to find out who's responsible for killing American soldiers. If Paramount Defense—or anyone associated with Project Olympus—is involved, I'll expose it, with or without your help."

For a moment, they locked eyes in a tense silence. Then, Briggs leaned back, his expression softening slightly. "I understand your position, Agent Hayes. But be warned—there are forces at work here that even I can't control. If you dig too deep, you might find yourself in over your head."

With that, Briggs picked up a folder on his desk, signaling that the conversation was over. Jack rose, giving the general one final, hard look before turning and leaving the office.

That evening, Jack returned to his quarters, his mind racing. He needed more information on Paramount Defense and their connection to Olympus. But official channels were limited; Briggs had made it clear that he wouldn't get any further cooperation from within the chain of command. That left him with one option—an unorthodox and dangerous one.

Jack had contacts on the dark web, a network of anonymous informants and former military personnel who dealt in information. It was a place for those who operated in the shadows, trading secrets that weren't meant to see the light of day. Jack's contact there was an elusive hacker known only as Cipher, a former NSA analyst who had turned rogue after uncovering government secrets that threatened her life.

Sitting at his laptop, Jack logged into a secure, encrypted chat platform, sending a message to Cipher.

> AgentH: Need a favor. Looking into Paramount Defense and a project called Olympus. Can you dig up anything?

He waited, his fingers drumming on the desk. After a few minutes, a reply flashed on the screen.

> Cipher: Long time, Jack. Olympus, huh? Big fish. I'll see what I can find.

A few hours later, a new message appeared.

> Cipher: Found a breadcrumb trail. There's talk on black sites about "Olympus" being linked to experimental weapons tech—some kind of prototype that's supposed to give a tactical edge. Paramount's been subcontracting for a piece of it. I'll send you a data packet, but be careful. The word on the dark net is, this tech could change warfare as we know it.

Jack downloaded the file Cipher sent, scrolling through the data. It included financial records, shipping manifests, and personnel reports linking Paramount Defense to various black-ops projects, many of which were marked "compromised." At least two dozen of the personnel involved had vanished without a trace in the last year alone, fueling rumors of assassinations and forced disappearances. Jack's stomach churned as he realized just how deep this conspiracy ran.

The final document caught his attention: an encrypted memo detailing an upcoming "field test" for Project Olympus, scheduled to take place in the same region where the ambush had occurred. The test, labeled "Operation Inferno," was slated for next month, with involvement from several high-ranking officials and representatives from Paramount Defense.

Jack leaned back, the pieces falling into place. The ambush hadn't just been an attack—it was a rehearsal. Whoever was behind this conspiracy wanted Olympus field-tested, and they didn't care how many lives were lost in the process.

Armed with this new information, Jack returned to his investigation with renewed urgency. He spent the next few days quietly interviewing soldiers, gathering data, and piecing together a timeline of events. Each conversation, each scrap of intel painted a clearer picture of the network operating behind the scenes, its tendrils reaching into every corner of the base.

From Lieutenant Mason's mention of unusual personnel activity to Specialist Monroe's intercepted transmission, each clue pointed to a carefully orchestrated scheme. Someone had provided real-time updates to the attackers during the ambush, and they'd done so with knowledge of the convoy's precise movements. It had to be someone within Outpost Grey—a mole embedded deep within the chain of command.

But the question remained: who?

Two days later, Jack received an anonymous message slipped under his door—a piece of paper with coordinates scrawled in neat handwriting, along with a single line of text:

"Sometimes, the best answer comes in the dark."

Chapter 6
Shadows in the Night

The night was silent, save for the soft hum of electrical equipment and the occasional clatter of boots as sentries patrolled Outpost Grey's perimeter. Jack Hayes stood outside his quarters, enveloped in the darkness, his eyes adjusting to the dim light of the distant searchlights. The air was crisp and still, and each exhale formed a faint cloud against the cold night.

Jack glanced down at the coordinates scribbled on the slip of paper he'd found under his door. They pointed to a location outside the base, a few miles east in the nearby hills—a dangerous area marked as restricted terrain, and frequented only by patrols. But whoever had left the note wanted him there for a reason, and if it was related to the ambush or Project Olympus, he couldn't ignore it.

Slipping the note into his pocket, Jack took a final look around to ensure he wasn't being watched, then set off toward the eastern edge of the base.

Jack had chosen his route carefully. The eastern edge of the base was bordered by dense underbrush and rugged terrain, providing cover for his departure. He'd dressed in all black, blending seamlessly with the shadows as he moved, ducking behind rocks and trees to avoid detection. The patrol schedule was ingrained in his mind; he knew exactly where each guard would be at this hour.

As he reached the fence, he pulled out a pair of wire cutters and quickly snipped a small section at the bottom, creating an opening just big enough to slide through. He paused, listening for any movement, and once he was sure the area was clear, he slipped through the fence and continued toward the coordinates.

The hills loomed ahead, silhouetted against the night sky, dark and foreboding. The path was rough, scattered with rocks and thorny shrubs, and Jack's boots crunched softly as he made his way up the incline. The climb was grueling, each step testing his balance and endurance. The air grew colder as he ascended, biting against his skin and making his breath hitch with each labored inhale.

After nearly an hour of climbing, he reached a small plateau, leveling out as he checked the coordinates again. He was close. Just a few more steps, and he would be there.

As Jack approached the designated coordinates, he spotted a faint glow up ahead—a dim flashlight, held low to the ground. His instincts screamed at him to be cautious; this could easily be a trap. He slowed his pace, moving with calculated precision, his hand resting on the grip of his concealed weapon as he closed the distance.

When he was close enough to see the figure holding the flashlight, he recognized them—a young woman in her mid-twenties, dressed in dark, nondescript clothing and a black cap that covered her hair. Her face was partially obscured by shadows, but Jack could see enough to recognize her as Specialist Lisa Monroe, the communications officer he'd interviewed just days before.

"Specialist Monroe," Jack whispered, his voice barely above a murmur. "You're the one who left the coordinates?"

She nodded, her expression tense and wary. "I couldn't risk speaking to you on base. Too many eyes and ears. But I have information—something you need to see."

Jack scanned their surroundings, making sure they were truly alone. "What kind of information?"

Monroe hesitated, glancing down at the flashlight before looking back up at him. "After the ambush, I kept monitoring the encrypted channels. There were more transmissions—encrypted ones—coming from within Outpost Grey. Whoever's behind this has been communicating with someone outside the base."

Jack's heart quickened. "Do you have any idea who's responsible?"

She shook her head. "I can't be certain, but I found one message that was left undeleted. I think... I think it was a mistake, left by someone who thought no one would notice."

She handed Jack a small, black USB drive, her fingers trembling slightly. "I managed to copy it before anyone could see. It contains the last transmission and its metadata. If you can decrypt it, it might tell us who's behind the leak."

Jack took the drive, examining it closely. This was exactly the break he needed, but it was also dangerous. Whoever was behind the transmissions had left it on base, meaning they could be watching both him and Monroe at any moment.

"Why did you decide to give this to me?" Jack asked, his voice soft.

Monroe looked down, her gaze pained. "I lost friends in that ambush, Agent Hayes. People I trained with, people I trusted. I couldn't just stand by and do nothing." She looked back up, her eyes filled with steely determination. "But you need to be careful. There's someone high up involved in this. They're covering their tracks."

Jack nodded, understanding the risk she had taken. "Thank you, Specialist Monroe. This might be exactly what I need to find out who's responsible."

Monroe nodded, her face tense. "I have to get back before anyone notices I'm gone. Just... be careful, Agent Hayes."

With that, she turned and disappeared into the shadows, leaving Jack alone with the drive in his hand and a growing sense of urgency.

Back at his quarters, Jack immediately set up a secure workstation, taking every precaution to prevent the signal from being traced. He plugged the USB drive into his laptop, launching a custom decryption tool he'd used in previous operations. The drive contained a single file—an encrypted audio recording, along with metadata showing the date, time, and location of the transmission.

The recording was recent, transmitted just days before the ambush. As Jack's decryption tool worked its way through the file, he reviewed the metadata, noting that the transmission had originated from a location on base, close to the restricted sections housing Project Olympus materials.

The decryption tool finished its work, and Jack played the audio. The recording was brief, filled with static, but a few words were clear enough to make out.

> "Proceed with the final phase. Target... convoy. Ensure... no survivors. Olympus remains secure."

The voice was distorted, scrambled to prevent identification, but the intent was unmistakable. This wasn't just an attack on a convoy; it was a calculated assassination, designed to eliminate anyone who might compromise Project Olympus.

Jack's mind raced, piecing together what he'd learned. This conspiracy was more insidious than he'd realized. The ambush hadn't been a one-off attack; it was part of a deliberate plan to silence anyone who might question Olympus's purpose. And whoever had given the order was on base, operating right under everyone's noses.

But why? What was so critical about Olympus that someone would go to such lengths to protect it?

Jack knew he needed answers fast. He decided to return to the analysis room to cross-check the metadata with recent personnel logs and radio traffic records. If he could match the time of the transmission to someone's movements, he might be able to identify the mole.

In the dim light of the analysis room, Jack poured over personnel records, meticulously combing through logs, access reports, and restricted area sign-ins. Each piece of data was a potential clue, a thread that might lead him closer to the truth. His mind raced with theories and suspicions, but none of them seemed to explain the extreme secrecy surrounding Olympus.

At last, he found a match.

On the night of the transmission, only a handful of personnel had accessed the restricted area, and among them was a name that jumped out—Captain Robert Langston. Jack remembered his earlier interview with Langston, the captain's defiant stance and barely concealed contempt for Project

Olympus. But if Langston was involved, his motives were still a mystery.

With mounting urgency, Jack decided to confront Langston directly. But as he prepared to leave the analysis room, he noticed something strange—his door was slightly ajar, despite locking it when he'd entered. The hairs on the back of his neck prickled as he reached for his weapon, moving silently toward the door.

Before he could reach it, the door swung open, and a figure stepped inside—a man dressed in plain fatigues with a face Jack didn't recognize. He held a silenced pistol, aimed directly at Jack.

"Agent Hayes," the man said, his voice low and steady. "You've been asking too many questions."

Jack's instincts took over. He ducked to the side just as the man fired, the silenced shot hitting the wall behind him. In a swift motion, Jack lunged at his attacker, grabbing his arm and twisting it as he forced the gun out of his hand. The two struggled in the cramped room, each fighting for control. The man was strong, trained, and relentless, but Jack's determination was stronger.

With a final surge of strength, Jack overpowered the attacker, slamming him against the desk and pinning him down. He pressed his own gun to the man's temple, his voice a low growl. "Who sent you?"

The man sneered, blood trickling from a cut on his lip. "You're in over your head, Hayes. Olympus isn't just a project—it's a new world order. And you can't stop it."

Before Jack could press further, the man twisted, biting down on something in his mouth. Within seconds, he convulsed violently, his body jerking as if caught in a death throe. His eyes bulged, and his breath came in ragged gasps, the last desperate moments of a man who knew the end was near. His hands clawed at his throat, but there was nothing to be done. His body went stiff, then slack, collapsing to the ground in a heap.

Jack stood frozen, watching the man's final moments play out in a surreal, almost slow-motion blur. The air around him felt thick, heavy with an unsettling stillness. For a moment, all that remained was the sound of Jack's heartbeat, pounding in his chest as if trying to escape. He glanced around the dim alley, instinctively reaching for his weapon, though it felt pointless. This man hadn't been killed by a bullet or a knife—he'd chosen death.

He'd bitten down on something. Jack's mind raced, but before he could make sense of it, the faint, acrid smell of poison reached his nostrils. A cyanide capsule. It was the only explanation. The man had been willing to die rather than let his secrets fall into Jack's hands.

As the final spasms of the man's body stilled, Jack's eyes moved to the shadows. He wasn't alone. There was someone else here. The figure moved in silence, their form barely visible in the dim light, but their presence was unmistakable—like a predator circling its prey.

Jack's hand moved to his side, instinctively grasping the cold steel of his weapon. "Who are you?" His voice was calm but sharp, demanding an answer.

The figure stepped forward slowly, revealing a tall, imposing woman. Her face was partially obscured by her dark hair, but her eyes were striking—icy and calculated. She surveyed the scene with cold disinterest, glancing briefly at the dead man before meeting Jack's gaze.

"You should have expected this," she said in a low voice. Her tone wasn't threatening, but there was an undeniable edge to it. "You've attracted attention."

Jack's grip on his weapon tightened. He didn't know who she was or what she wanted, but one thing was clear: This wasn't over. The real danger was just beginning.

"Who sent you?" he demanded, though deep down he feared the answer.

Chapter 7
The Deepening Web

The room was heavy with tension as Jack stood over the body of the man he had just subdued. The dim light from his desk lamp illuminated the cold, lifeless face of the intruder. He had barely spoken before biting down on the cyanide capsule hidden beneath his tongue, a last-ditch effort to take his secrets to the grave. The bitter, acrid scent of poison filled the air, a stark reminder of the danger Jack was now embroiled in.

Jack wiped the sweat from his brow, his heart pounding as the adrenaline continued to surge through him. His pulse echoed in his ears, drowning out the noise of his thoughts. For a moment, he just stood there, staring at the dead man. He had hoped the confrontation would bring clarity, but now it only deepened the mystery. Who had sent this man to kill him? And why had he been so determined to silence Jack?

The man's military fatigues suggested he was part of the base's security detail, but there was no clear indication of rank or unit. His gear was unremarkable, but his calm demeanor and lethal efficiency suggested a well-trained operative. Whoever he was, he wasn't just a random assassin; he was part of something larger. Something connected to Project Olympus.

Jack turned his attention back to the USB drive Monroe had given him. The encrypted file still burned in his mind. The voice on the transmission—the message of "final phase," "convoy," and

"Olympus"—told him that whoever was behind this wasn't just concerned with military security. This was a calculated, high-level operation, orchestrated by forces beyond the ordinary chain of command. Someone in the upper echelons of power was pulling strings, and Jack was getting closer to the heart of it.

By the time Jack had disposed of the body and scrubbed the room clean of any evidence, it was already dawn. He sat at his desk, exhausted but driven, as he sifted through the intel he had gathered so far. The encrypted file Monroe had provided was at the top of the list, but he needed more—something concrete that would connect the dots between the ambush, Project Olympus, and the men and women responsible for it.

The computer screen flickered to life as Jack opened the personnel file for Captain Robert Langston, the officer whose name had popped up in the metadata of the transmission. Langston had served in a variety of special operations units before being assigned to Outpost Grey. His record was impeccable, with commendations for bravery and exceptional leadership in the field. Yet Jack knew there was more to him than what appeared on paper.

He found a file labeled "Classified – Operation Olympus: Langston's Involvement." As Jack opened the document, his eyes narrowed at the first few lines. Langston was listed as a senior officer within the Olympus program—someone deeply embedded in the project's covert operations. The file detailed his involvement in various high-risk assignments, including missions in conflict zones where casualties were often high and objectives unclear. There was even mention of his presence during some of the more clandestine operations involving Paramount Defense.

But it was the final line of the document that stopped Jack dead in his tracks.

> "Captain Langston has been flagged for suspicion regarding unauthorized communications with outside entities. Pending further investigation."

Jack's stomach churned. Langston had been flagged as a potential leak, someone with connections outside the military—a traitor, possibly. This wasn't just about Olympus or the ambush. It was about something much bigger—an operation to control and manipulate, to conduct covert warfare on a scale Jack hadn't even imagined. Langston could be the key to everything.

But why would Langston try to kill him? Had he caught wind of Jack's investigation and decided to eliminate the threat? Or was Jack getting too close to the truth?

Before Jack could process the implications, his phone buzzed. It was a secure message from Monroe.

> Monroe: "Get out. Langston knows you're digging. He's tracking your movements. Don't trust anyone. I've found something else. Meet me at the old barracks, 2200 hours."

Jack stared at the message for a long time, his mind racing. Monroe had just confirmed his worst fear: Langston was onto him. If Langston was indeed compromised, Jack was now a target. The fact that she was still willing to meet him, despite the danger, spoke volumes about her loyalty. But this was no longer just about Project Olympus. It was a war—one in which Jack had unwittingly become a pawn.

He had no time to waste. Langston was resourceful, and the man who had tried to kill him the previous night was proof that the conspirators were watching his every move. Jack needed to be smarter than ever before. He couldn't afford to make any mistakes.

Jack grabbed his gear, carefully checking his weapon and communications equipment. He erased all traces of his investigation from the base's secure servers, making sure there would be no evidence linking him to the files or the message from Monroe. It was becoming clear that Outpost Grey was no longer a safe place for him to operate. If Langston was truly compromised, there was no one on the base he could trust.

As he made his way out of his quarters and into the dim, quiet hallways of the base, Jack couldn't shake the feeling that this was all part of a larger plan. The ambush, the mysterious communication, the men hunting him—everything was falling into place like pieces of a deadly puzzle. And now, he was caught in the middle of it.

The old barracks sat on the edge of Outpost Grey, abandoned for years and rarely used. The building's peeling paint and broken windows gave it an eerie, haunted quality. Jack had been there once, years ago, during a training exercise. It was the perfect place for a secret meeting—isolated and out of the way.

As he approached the barracks, Jack noticed the telltale sign that someone had been there recently—fresh footprints in the dirt leading to the side entrance. He was not alone.

He moved cautiously, slipping through the shadows, his every sense on high alert. He knew Langston's men could be anywhere. The soldiers stationed at Outpost Grey were well-trained, and Langston had access to every corner of the base. Jack's heart pounded in his chest as he made his way into the building.

The interior of the barracks was just as rundown as the outside. Old military gear was scattered around, cobwebs hanging from the rafters, and the smell of mildew filled the air. Jack moved silently through the building, his eyes scanning every corner for any sign of movement.

Suddenly, a soft voice echoed from the shadows.

"Agent Hayes," Monroe said, stepping out from behind a pillar. "I knew you'd come."

Jack tensed, his hand instinctively going to his weapon, but then he relaxed when he saw Monroe's face. She looked just as determined as she had the night before, though her eyes were filled with worry. She motioned for him to follow her as she turned down a narrow hallway.

"What did you find?" Jack whispered.

Monroe glanced around, making sure no one was nearby. "I've been going through the Olympus files—hidden documents, encrypted messages, everything I could get my hands on. What I found... it's not just about weapons, Jack. Olympus is a cover for something far darker."

Jack's brow furrowed as he followed her into a small, abandoned storage room. She quickly closed the door behind them and locked it. The air inside was thick, the only light coming from a flickering overhead bulb.

"What do you mean?" Jack asked.

Monroe's voice dropped to a whisper. "I found evidence of biological warfare research—experiments with genetic modification and weaponized pathogens. They've been testing these weapons in real-world environments, in civilian populations. The project isn't just about military superiority. It's about controlling entire populations. Creating soldiers—perfect soldiers—by altering their DNA."

Jack's mind reeled at the implications. "Are you saying that Project Olympus is developing bioweapons?"

Monroe nodded grimly. "Yes, and worse. They've been conducting trials on people—on civilians. They've already tested it in several regions, and the results are... horrifying."

Jack's heart sank. "This goes far beyond anything I imagined."

Monroe lowered her voice even further. "Langston's involvement in Olympus isn't just because he's a loyal officer. He's been working with Paramount Defense to supply the research facilities with human subjects, people who were abducted and used in these experiments. They've been silencing anyone who gets too close to the truth."

Jack was silent for a long moment, the weight of her words sinking in. Everything he had uncovered—the ambush, the mysterious transmission, the attempts on his life—had all led to this. Project Olympus was far more sinister than he had ever imagined. And now, it was no longer just a matter of stopping an enemy attack—it was a race against time to stop a global catastrophe.

But who could he trust? And what would it take to stop an operation so deeply entrenched within the highest levels of power?

Before Jack could respond, Monroe's eyes flicked to the door, her face Before Jack could respond, Monroe's eyes flicked to the door, her face tight with fear. The unmistakable sound of footsteps echoed through the hallway, growing louder by the second. Someone was coming.

Jack's hand instinctively went to his weapon, but Monroe stopped him with a subtle shake of her head. They needed information, not a fight—not yet. They weren't ready for Langston's men to descend upon them.

"We have to move. Now," Monroe whispered urgently.

Jack nodded, his heart racing, and they both crouched low, blending into the shadows. The footsteps were nearly upon them. They could hear muffled voices, the sound of boots against the floor. It was only a matter of seconds before Langston's forces would burst through the door.

Monroe and Jack exchanged a tense glance. They had no choice but to make a run for it, to escape and regroup. But the question remained: How much longer could they stay one step ahead of Langston and his network?

The race was on, and the stakes had never been higher.

Chapter 8
The Edge of War

The sterile, high-tech room hummed with the quiet sound of machinery, but for Jack Hayes, it felt suffocating. He stood face to face with Captain Robert Langston, flanked by two armed security officers, all of them standing in the heart of Project Olympus. The air was thick with tension, the reality of the situation closing in around him like a vice.

Langston's smile was cold, calculated, his eyes glinting with something dark. His posture was that of a man who knew he had already won. The well-pressed uniform, the calm confidence—everything about him screamed authority, and it was clear that Langston believed he was untouchable.

"You've been a thorn in my side for far too long, Hayes," Langston said, his voice carrying a quiet menace. "You should've left well enough alone. Now, you and Monroe are going to watch as everything you've worked for unravels."

Monroe stiffened beside Jack, her eyes flashing with defiance. But she said nothing. She knew better than to provoke Langston in such a moment of vulnerability. The guards flanking Langston held their weapons with military precision, ready to strike at the slightest command. The room was a trap, and they were caught in the center of it.

Jack's mind was racing, but he forced himself to stay calm. His instincts were screaming at him to act, but there was no easy way out. He knew the only way to stop Langston was to expose him for what he truly was—the mastermind behind a covert operation that had the potential to change the world, for better or for worse.

"Langston," Jack said, his voice steady but hard. "You don't have to do this. We can stop all of this, but it has to end now. Whatever you're involved in with Paramount Defense, whatever you've been hiding—there's still time to make things right."

Langston's smile faded slightly, and his eyes narrowed. "Make things right?" he repeated. "You still don't understand, do you? There's no going back from this. Olympus is already beyond your reach. It's not about making things right. It's about ensuring that humanity survives. That we, the few who are worthy, control the future."

Jack's blood ran cold. The conviction in Langston's voice sent a chill down his spine. Langston wasn't just a soldier or a rogue officer; he was an architect of a vision—a terrifying one, but one he believed was necessary for the future of mankind.

"Survive?" Monroe spat, her voice sharp. "You're talking about mass control, genetic manipulation, biological warfare. How many innocent lives have you destroyed just to fulfill your twisted vision? This isn't survival, Langston. It's genocide."

Langston's lips curled into a sneer, and his eyes flicked briefly to the guards behind him. "You think I'm the villain in this story? You think I'm the one destroying lives? You have no idea what's at stake. You've been in the dark this entire time, running blind, but I—" He paused, gathering his thoughts with the smug assurance of a man who had already convinced himself he was right. "I've seen the future. I've seen what happens when the weak inherit the Earth. When the unfit have control. Olympus is the answer to a world in chaos. We will create a new order, a new kind of soldier, a new breed of human. One that is stronger, more resilient, more adaptable."

Jack and Monroe exchanged a glance. The reality of what Langston was saying hit them both like a punch to the gut. Langston wasn't just some rogue officer; he was the architect of a monstrous vision. And that vision wasn't just about weapons—it was about reshaping humanity itself. Through experimentation, genetic alteration, and ruthless population control, Langston intended to create a new species—one that could survive whatever storm was coming, even if it meant destroying those who were "unfit."

"Monroe," Jack said quietly, his gaze never leaving Langston, "tell me again about the biological research. The human trials. Everything you found."

Monroe, ever the professional, didn't flinch. She steadied herself and replied, "Langston's been working with Paramount Defense and other private contractors, running secret experiments on civilians in remote areas. They've been manipulating DNA, engineering soldiers that can withstand radiation, disease, and even psychological trauma. They're using the population as test subjects, Jack. And Langston has been covering it up with military protocol, presenting it as a 'security measure.'"

Langston laughed, a low, mocking sound. "You don't understand anything, do you? You still think this is about right and wrong. It's not. It's about survival of the fittest. And you, Hayes, are nothing but a roadblock."

Jack's blood boiled at the callousness of Langston's words, but he kept his composure. "Then why go after us? Why silence us if you believe in this so much?"

Langston's face hardened. "Because you've gotten too close to the truth, Hayes. I've been watching your every move. You and Monroe, your investigation—it was always a threat to me, to the plan. And now, you're too far in. You think you can expose me? You think anyone will believe you? You're just one man, fighting a battle you can't win."

The guards began to move closer, their weapons raised slightly. Jack's instincts screamed at him that this was the moment when everything would explode into chaos. Langston, it seemed, had grown tired of the conversation. He had no intention of negotiating, no intention of giving Jack or Monroe a way out. They were dead, in his eyes—just obstacles to be cleared.

Without warning, the sound of gunfire shattered the tense silence.

Jack's heart skipped a beat, but the gunfire wasn't directed at them. It came from somewhere deeper inside the facility—distant, but distinct. The doors to the facility's control room had been breached. Someone was already inside. Someone who had come to stop Langston.

"What's going on?" Langston barked, his voice filled with frustration and disbelief. He turned toward the sound of the gunfire, his face twisted with anger. "No one was supposed to be here. No one knew—"

Jack's pulse quickened. This was it. The opportunity they needed.

"Monroe, now!" Jack shouted.

In an instant, Monroe sprinted toward the far corner of the room, ducking behind a stack of crates. Jack drew his weapon, moving quickly toward the center of the room, and Langston's men reacted with lethal efficiency. They were well-trained, but they weren't prepared for the chaos that erupted in the next few seconds.

The gunfire grew louder, closer, and Jack realized with shock that the noise wasn't just from a few operatives—it was a full-scale assault. Someone had breached the perimeter, and they weren't here to take prisoners.

"Langston!" Jack yelled, using the chaos as cover to close the distance. "This is over. It's not just you anymore. You can't control this."

Langston whirled around, his face a mask of fury and disbelief. "You think you can stop me, Hayes? You're nothing but a pawn in a game you don't even understand."

But before Langston could react further, the facility's main power grid suddenly cut out, plunging them all into darkness.

For a split second, everything was chaos. Gunshots rang out, the sound of movement was deafening, and the sound of the facility's emergency alarms blared in the background. Jack's heart pounded in his chest as he scanned the darkened room, trying to locate Monroe and the source of the gunfire.

Monroe's voice cut through the chaos. "Jack! Behind you!"

Jack spun just in time to see Langston's final strike. Langston, desperate to take control, had drawn a sidearm and was moving toward him with dangerous precision.

But before Langston could fire, a single shot rang out from the darkness, and Langston crumpled to the floor, his weapon falling from his hand.

The room fell silent.

Jack turned to see a figure emerging from the shadows. The silhouette of a man, tall, wearing tactical gear—someone who wasn't supposed to be here, but who had just saved their lives.

"Who the hell are you?" Jack demanded, his hand still clutching his gun.

The figure lowered his weapon and stepped forward, his face illuminated by the dim emergency lights. He was older than Jack, grizzled, with scars on his face that spoke of years spent in combat.

"I'm here to finish what you started, Hayes," the man said, his voice low and gravelly. "Langston was just the beginning. Olympus is much bigger than you think."

Jack felt a surge of mixed emotions—relief, confusion, and fear all battling for dominance. This wasn't just the end of Langston. This was the beginning of something far larger.

The man introduced himself as General Victor Hayes, a former high-ranking officer who had gone rogue years ago after uncovering the true nature of Olympus. He had been working against Langston and the program for years, but in secret.

Chapter 9
The War Within

The silence in the room was deafening. After Langston had fallen, the tension hadn't lifted, and the storm outside seemed to mirror the chaos brewing inside the Olympus facility. Jack's grip tightened around his weapon as he took in the sight of General Victor Hayes—an older man with the kind of hardened military presence that spoke of years of blood, sweat, and warfare. He had just saved their lives, but now, a deeper, more pressing question echoed in Jack's mind.

Who is this man?

Victor didn't wait for Jack's response. He turned, his sharp gaze moving over Langston's body on the floor and then to Monroe, who had stayed behind cover, eyeing the situation carefully.

"We don't have much time," Victor said, his voice low but commanding. "Langston's death won't stop the machine. They'll send a cleanup team within minutes. And Olympus isn't just here. It's spread across the globe. They've activated the final phase, and if we don't act now, it's over."

Jack's heart skipped a beat. The urgency in Victor's tone wasn't just a command—it was a warning. Langston's death might have ended the man's twisted grip on Olympus, but the operation itself was far from over. If anything, it was about to enter its final phase.

Monroe cautiously emerged from her hiding spot, her face pale but determined. She nodded toward the body on the floor. "You said they'd send a cleanup crew. Does that mean Langston wasn't running this show alone?"

Victor's eyes darkened, and for a moment, Jack saw something in his gaze—a flicker of regret, or perhaps recognition, before it was quickly hidden.

"No, he wasn't alone," Victor replied, his voice grim. "Langston was just the puppet, the figurehead. The true power behind Olympus is a covert military-industrial alliance—a conglomerate of defense contractors, tech giants, and shadow governments. They control everything. Langston had no choice but to follow orders. The cleanup crew you're about to face? They're not regular soldiers. They're the elite, sent in to tie up loose ends. And you two have just become their number one target."

Jack exhaled slowly, his mind racing. A covert military-industrial alliance? That was bigger than anything he had anticipated. The threat wasn't just one rogue officer or an isolated project. This was global. Olympus wasn't just a rogue operation. It was an insidious machine that had been allowed to grow, hidden under layers of secrecy, and it had spread far beyond the confines of a single base.

"And you're just telling us this now?" Jack asked, his tone sharp, though he couldn't afford to waste time on anger. "What's your stake in all of this, General?"

Victor met his gaze without flinching. "My stake?" He smiled bitterly. "I've been fighting this war for years. Langston was part of it, but he was always a pawn. The real enemy... they're still out there. And they'll stop at nothing to see Olympus through to completion."

Monroe's brow furrowed. "What does Olympus actually do, General? You've been vague about that. You're talking about genetic experiments, mind control, bioweapons. But what's the endgame? What are they planning to do with all this?"

Victor paused, as if weighing how much to reveal. Then, finally, his voice dropped to a near-whisper, full of grim resolve.

"Olympus isn't just about creating soldiers or weapons—it's about creating a new world order. A world where the people in charge control every aspect of society, every system. They've been working in the shadows for decades. The 'new breed' Langston talked about isn't just for war—it's for control. They've been experimenting on civilians, creating genetically modified super-soldiers, immune to disease, capable of surviving in the harshest environments. But the real endgame? They want to make an army of humans who are completely subservient, able to be controlled through technology. Not just soldiers—citizens. Imagine a world where every move, every thought, is monitored and influenced. Where governments, corporations, and military powers combine into one unified force with the power to reshape the world."

The weight of Victor's words hung in the air like a shroud. Jack felt as though the floor had been ripped out from under him. They weren't just facing a military operation anymore. They were fighting a war for the very soul of humanity itself.

Jack's voice was barely a whisper. "That's insane. No one would allow it. People would rebel."

Victor's expression remained somber. "That's where the final phase comes in. They've perfected the neural implant system, the technology that will allow them to control the population on a global scale. The technology was tested in select cities, and it's ready to be deployed worldwide. Once it's live, there's no turning back. The rebellion you're talking about? It won't happen. The moment the implant activates, it will override any resistance. It's already been deployed in key regions. The clock is ticking, and once they activate the satellites, the system will go live globally."

Jack felt the blood drain from his face. It was worse than he imagined. Langston's project was not just a military initiative—it was the beginning of a terrifying future where the elite would control every aspect of life. And it was all coming to a head now.

"But we can stop it, right?" Monroe's voice was full of determination. "We can take down the satellites, destroy the system, right?"

Victor's gaze flicked to Monroe, a look of understanding passing between them. He knew what she was asking, and for a moment, he hesitated.

"We can try," he said, his voice heavy with the burden of the truth. "But the facility here is just one of many. The real control center is miles away, in a bunker beneath a facility in Cedar Springs, Colorado. If we're going to have any chance of stopping them, we have to reach that facility and destroy the mainframe that links everything together. If we don't, all of this—it's over."

The words hung in the air, and for a moment, everything seemed insurmountable. Cedar Springs. The heart of the operation. The final phase. The place where they would either end it all or see humanity plunge into a dark future of control and subjugation.

Monroe spoke first, her voice steady despite the weight of their task. "How do we get to Cedar Springs without getting caught? If Langston's cleanup crew is already on their way, we're running out of time."

Victor didn't hesitate. "I have a network of contacts—old allies from my days in the service. They'll get us out of here, provide us with transport. But we have to move fast. The facility will go into lockdown once the word gets out that Langston is dead. We'll need to slip out unnoticed and get to a safe house, regroup, and plan our next move."

Jack nodded, knowing that every second counted. But as they prepared to leave the room, a loud clang echoed from down the hallway. It was the unmistakable sound of heavy boots—soldiers, and they were coming fast.

"We don't have much time," Jack said. "Victor, you're sure about the way out?"

Victor's eyes narrowed, his military training kicking in as he scanned the situation. "The rear exit is the best shot. There's an old service tunnel under this wing of the building. We can take that route to avoid detection."

Monroe drew her own weapon, her gaze focused and alert. "Let's move. We can talk strategy once we're out of here."

They moved quickly, slipping through the facility's corridors with precision. Jack's thoughts raced ahead. They had to make it to Cedar Springs—had to stop the final phase before it was too late. As they passed through the maintenance hallways, the eerie stillness was broken by the sound of distant alarms, signaling that the facility had been breached. Langston's death had set the countdown in motion, and now the facility was in full lockdown.

Victor led them through a series of dimly lit corridors, finally arriving at a reinforced door that led to the service tunnel. As they approached, a crackling voice came over the facility's intercom.

"Attention all personnel. Code Red has been initiated. All units proceed to Sector Alpha immediately. Failure to comply will result in termination."

Monroe tensed, her fingers curling around her weapon. "They're locking everything down. We need to get out, now."

Victor didn't waste a second. He swiped a keycard on the door's control panel, and with a soft hiss, the door slid open. "Move!"

They rushed through the tunnel, the echo of their footsteps merging with the frantic beeping of the facility's lockdown systems. Jack could feel the weight of their mission bearing down on him. They had one shot—one opportunity to stop Olympus and prevent the global takeover Langston had set in motion.

As they emerged into the cold night air, Jack knew the real battle had only just begun. And now, they had to survive long enough to make it to Cedar Springs—or risk everything.

Chapter 10
Into the Fire

The cold night air bit at their skin as they emerged from the tunnel into the darkness. The Olympus facility behind them was locked down tighter than ever, and the alarm systems blared through the facility's corridors, signaling the gravity of the situation. Jack's heart pounded, each step echoing in his ears as they sprinted toward the waiting vehicles. The world outside was stark and quiet, the moon casting long shadows across the sprawling landscape. But the calm was an illusion—inside, everything was unraveling.

Victor led the way, his years of military experience evident in his swift, purposeful movements. He knew the terrain well. There was no room for hesitation. The enemy would be closing in soon, and their only chance to survive was to get to Cedar Springs, where they could disable the system that powered Olympus. If they failed, everything was lost.

Jack's thoughts were a whirlwind as he kept pace, scanning their surroundings. It was hard to believe that just hours ago, they were inside the very building that had held the key to everything—Langston's twisted project, the experiments, the surveillance state. They had been so close to falling into his grasp, but now they were free. At least for the moment.

Monroe was beside him, her eyes sharp as ever, her fingers lightly brushing the weapon at her side. She was a master of keeping calm under pressure, but Jack could see the storm brewing behind her calm demeanor. She understood the magnitude of what they were facing.

"Victor," Monroe said, her voice low but full of urgency, "what's our plan? We can't just drive into Cedar Springs and hope for the best. Langston's people—this entire operation—they're too well-funded, too connected. We need to be strategic."

Victor glanced over his shoulder, his eyes flicking to the sky as though gauging the situation. "You're right. They'll be tracking us. There's a way to throw them off our trail, but it'll take time. We need to get to Blackstone Ridge. It's an old safehouse—a network of underground bunkers hidden from satellite surveillance. There, we can regroup and plan the next phase."

Jack nodded. They had no choice. Every moment spent in the open was a risk. The weight of their mission bore down on him like a physical force. Cedar Springs wasn't just another military base. It was the last line of defense for Olympus, the control center where they would activate the final phase of their operation—a satellite system that would broadcast mind-controlling signals across the globe.

But getting there would mean navigating through hostile territory, evading detection, and taking down enemies who had no qualms about eliminating anyone who stood in their way.

As they neared the makeshift vehicles—a collection of old military jeeps hidden beneath tarps—Victor didn't hesitate. He motioned for them to climb into the lead vehicle. Monroe jumped into the passenger seat, checking her weapons one last time. Jack slid into the back, pulling the seatbelt across his chest and leaning forward as he addressed Victor.

"Do you have any idea how many people are involved in this operation?" Jack asked, his voice tight with suppressed tension.

Victor's hands gripped the wheel as he started the engine. "Too many to count. Olympus has been in the works for over two decades. From the top military brass to corporate giants in Silicon Valley. Even certain political figures have been compromised. There's no one left who's free of their influence. But it's not just about power—it's about control. They want to be the ones who shape the future, and they'll do anything to get it."

Jack clenched his jaw. "And we're the ones standing in their way."

Victor didn't respond immediately, his eyes focused on the road ahead. The vehicle bounced over the rough terrain as they sped away from the facility. "Yes. But we're not alone. The resistance is bigger than you think. We just have to get to Cedar Springs and activate the countermeasure systems. If we can disable the satellite communications, we'll cripple the Olympus operation."

Monroe, ever the pragmatist, raised an eyebrow. "That's a big if. And what makes you think we're going to make it there in one piece?"

Victor gave her a hard look, the kind that said he understood the stakes. "Because we don't have a choice. This is the last chance we'll get. If we don't make it, the world as you know it will be gone."

The weight of his words settled over them as the landscape outside blurred into the night. They were heading into enemy territory, and the further they traveled, the more Jack felt the magnitude of what was at stake. Cedar Springs was their last hope. But every road, every turn they took felt like an invitation to death.

The journey to Blackstone Ridge was treacherous, not just because of the terrain, but because of the constant risk of being detected. Victor's vehicle swerved around sharp turns and over rugged hills, expertly avoiding the roads that could be monitored by satellites or local patrols. The world outside was a blur of snow-covered trees and darkened mountains, but the tension inside the jeep was palpable.

"We can't afford to stop," Monroe said, her voice sharp. "Even for fuel. If they're tracking us, we'll give away our position."

Victor nodded in agreement, his eyes scanning the rearview mirror. "I know. But we have a few miles before we hit the first roadblock. We'll make it."

Jack stared out the window, his thoughts drifting back to the events that had led them here. He couldn't shake the images of the facility—the experiments, the innocent lives destroyed, the soldiers who had been unknowingly altered for Langston's vision. It made his stomach churn. The horror of what Olympus had become was too vast to grasp in one sitting, but the weight of their responsibility felt heavier with each passing mile.

As they drove deeper into the mountains, Jack knew that time was running out. Even if they reached Blackstone Ridge, there was still the task of infiltrating Cedar Springs, of getting past the fortified defenses, and then the real battle—disabling the satellite system. There was no room for error.

The engine of the jeep rumbled steadily, but the silence between them was thick with anticipation.

Finally, after hours of tense driving, they arrived at a small, isolated mountain range. Victor slowed the jeep to a crawl, pulling off the main trail and into a narrow path that wound its way through dense trees. Jack's senses were on high alert. Every snap of a twig, every distant noise, felt like an alarm.

Victor pulled the jeep to a stop in front of a small cabin, nestled discreetly into the hillside. It looked abandoned—quiet, almost eerie—but to Jack's trained eye, it was a perfect hideout.

"This is Blackstone Ridge," Victor said, his voice calm but with a note of urgency. "The safehouse. We'll stay here for a few hours to regroup and finalize our plan. We need to rest and be ready. The real fight begins when we hit Cedar Springs."

Jack, Monroe, and Victor climbed out of the jeep, checking their weapons one last time as they approached the cabin. The doors creaked as Victor pushed them open, revealing a dimly lit interior, furnished only with the essentials: a small kitchen, a few chairs, and a couple of makeshift cots. It wasn't much, but it was enough.

"Alright," Victor said, locking the door behind them. "We need to get some rest. I'll set up the communications equipment. We need to contact our allies and get a clear picture of what's happening on the ground. Monroe, Jack—get some food, and we'll strategize after."

Monroe immediately began checking their supplies, grabbing cans of food and a bottle of water. Jack took a seat at the small table, still unable to shake the sense of urgency gnawing at him.

"We can't afford to wait too long," Jack muttered. "Langston's people are relentless. The cleanup crew won't stop until we're dead."

Victor, who had been setting up a satellite phone, paused and turned toward him. His face was grim, but there was a fire in his eyes—a determination that mirrored Jack's own.

"We won't be waiting long. But once we hit Cedar Springs, there's no turning back. If we can't stop Olympus there, we're all finished."

As the weight of the mission settled over them like a thick fog, Jack realized that this was no longer just about stopping an operation. It was about preventing the dawn of a new world—one where freedom was no longer a choice. Where every citizen was controlled by an invisible hand, their every thought and action dictated by the power of Olympus.

Jack looked at Monroe, then Victor. The time for hesitation was over. They were about to enter the heart of Olympus itself, where the stakes had never been higher.

"We're ready," Jack said, his voice steady, despite the fear simmering beneath.

Victor met his gaze with a nod. "Then let's end this."

Chapter 11
The Heart of Olympus

The winds howled through the mountain pass as Jack, Monroe, and Victor made their way toward Cedar Springs. The safehouse at Blackstone Ridge had served its purpose, offering a brief respite from the relentless pursuit of Olympus's forces. But as they packed up and prepared to head out, the weight of their task loomed larger than ever. Every step closer to their destination felt heavier, each mile stretching the thin thread of hope they clung to.

Victor led them through the winding mountain roads, the landscape growing more desolate as they neared their objective. The rugged terrain was an advantage, providing a natural barrier, but it was also a double-edged sword. Cedar Springs was a well-guarded military compound, hidden beneath layers of surveillance, fortified structures, and high-tech security systems.

The facility, designed to look like an innocuous research station on the outside, had been repurposed for something far darker. The satellite systems it housed weren't just for communication—they were the backbone of Project Olympus, capable of overriding entire populations' minds. It was a weaponized vision of control, one that would redefine the concept of freedom.

As the jeep slowed, Victor motioned for them to stop. They had arrived at the edge of Cedar Springs, the snow-dusted cliffs looming like a jagged wall. A few hundred yards ahead, the facility was visible, its exterior a blend of military-grade architecture and high-tech surveillance equipment.

"We need to be cautious," Victor said, his voice low but resolute. "The moment we enter the facility, we're no longer dealing with ordinary soldiers. These people are trained to protect the core of Olympus, and they won't hesitate to kill us on sight. You both know what we're up against."

Monroe adjusted her weapon, a flash of determination in her eyes. "I didn't come this far to back down now."

Jack nodded, glancing at the facility ahead. Every instinct told him that this would be the hardest part of the mission. They had to infiltrate Cedar Springs without triggering the alarms. If they alerted the facility to their presence, they'd be dead before they could reach the main control room. There was no margin for error.

"Let's move," Victor said, signaling for them to follow.

Creeping through the dense trees that surrounded Cedar Springs, the team moved like shadows in the night. The moon hung high above them, casting pale light on the snow, but they kept their movements slow and deliberate, knowing any sound could betray them. The snow crunched beneath their boots, but Victor had planned for this—the path they were following was shielded by natural terrain and a few clever detours he had learned from his days in the service.

Jack's senses were heightened. His mind raced with every possible scenario—what would happen if they were spotted? How could they disable the systems without being overwhelmed by security? Each step brought them closer to the heart of Olympus, but the tension in the air was thick enough to cut.

They passed the first guard tower without incident, a silent patrol moving past them unaware. But as they drew nearer to the central compound, the atmosphere grew heavier, more oppressive. The facility loomed larger, surrounded by layers of electronic fences and laser grids. It was clear that security was not just a priority—it was the core of their defense.

"We need to find a way inside without being seen," Monroe murmured, scanning the perimeter.

Victor, who had been in quiet communication with his contacts, pulled out a small device from his jacket. "There's a maintenance hatch on the far side. It's not monitored as heavily as the main entrances, and it leads directly to the sublevels where the satellite controls are housed. But we'll need to move quickly. Once we're in, there's no turning back."

Jack exchanged a glance with Monroe. "Let's do it."

Once inside the maintenance hatch, the trio descended into a maze of tunnels, illuminated only by the flickering lights overhead. The smell of dust and rust filled the air, and the echo of their footsteps reverberated off the cold concrete walls. Despite the eerie silence, there was an underlying hum—something mechanical, alive, and dangerous.

Victor led them deeper into the complex, moving swiftly but carefully. He had memorized the layout of the facility, the same way soldiers memorize the layout of a battlefield. The further they went, the more palpable the danger became. It wasn't just the armed guards or the advanced surveillance—it was the fear that gripped Jack's heart. The deeper they went, the closer they got to the beating heart of Project Olympus.

The path finally opened into a large chamber, a sprawling command center that stretched in all directions. Monitors blinked with streams of data, and servers hummed as if they were alive, processing vast amounts of information. It was overwhelming—the kind of control the system had over information, over people, over entire nations. The scale of it was unlike anything Jack had ever imagined.

In the center of the room, a massive control console dominated the space. It was surrounded by rows of advanced computers, each linked to satellites orbiting miles above them. The air was thick with tension as Jack and Monroe approached, but it wasn't the satellites that made Jack's skin crawl—it was what they saw on the screens.

On the central monitor, a live feed displayed several cities across the globe—massive crowds of people milling about, unaware of the presence of the satellites overhead. But the chilling part? The screens were tracking them—counting them, analyzing their movements. The technology was watching every person, every face, every motion. It was a living, breathing system of control.

And it was only moments away from activation.

"This is it," Victor whispered, his voice tinged with a mixture of awe and dread. "This is what they've been working toward all these years. They've already begun deploying the neural implants across key populations. The satellites are ready. Once they activate, it's over."

Jack felt the weight of Victor's words sink in. The enemy wasn't just aiming to control governments or military forces. They were after something far more insidious—total, absolute control over the people themselves.

Monroe's voice cut through the heavy silence. "How do we stop it?"

Victor walked toward the main console, his fingers brushing over the control panels. "We need to get to the core system—disable the satellites and cut off their access to the neural networks. If we can destroy the central server, it will disable the entire system. But we need to move quickly. The countdown has already begun. Once the satellites are activated, the global network will be live within minutes."

Just as he finished speaking, the sound of footsteps echoed from the hallway. Jack's instincts kicked in. They weren't alone.

Victor's eyes widened. "It's a trap."

The team quickly scattered, ducking behind server racks and control consoles. They had underestimated how quickly the facility would respond. The doors to the control room slammed open, and a group of armed soldiers rushed in, guns raised. At their head stood a figure Jack instantly recognized—General Langston.

But this time, Langston wasn't alone. He was flanked by several high-ranking military officers—men and women who had been deeply embedded in Olympus's operations from the start. Their faces were cold, calculating. They weren't just soldiers; they were the architects of this new world order.

"Well, well," Langston said with a smirk, his voice cold and detached. "It seems we have some unexpected visitors."

Jack's heart pounded in his chest as Langston's gaze swept over the room, locking eyes with Victor. There was no surprise in Langston's eyes, only a cruel, predatory satisfaction. "I knew you'd come eventually. But you're too late. The satellites are already in position, and the broadcast will begin shortly. You're not stopping anything."

Victor stepped forward, his own weapon raised, but his voice was calm, resolute. "You're wrong, Langston. It's not too late. We're shutting this down."

Langston laughed, the sound cold and empty. "You still don't understand, do you? It was never about just controlling soldiers or politicians. It's about controlling the future. Once the system is live, it'll be impossible to reverse. The people won't fight. They'll be under my control. Every thought, every action—controlled."

Monroe's eyes narrowed. "We'll see about that."

The tension in the room thickened as the standoff continued. Guns were drawn, and the soldiers surrounding Langston shifted their positions, waiting for an order. But Jack, Victor, and Monroe were no longer just trying to survive—they were trying to destroy the very system that threatened the future of humanity.

Victor fired first, taking out one of Langston's officers before ducking behind a column. Jack and Monroe followed suit, returning fire as they sprinted toward the central console.

Langston's face twisted with rage. "You think you can stop this? You've already lost!"

But as Langston spoke, the team's coordinated attack began to take effect. The security systems faltered, the screens flickered, and the countdown timer on the central console began to reset. They were getting closer.

In the chaos, Jack saw a glimmer of hope. But Langston wasn't finished yet. He charged forward, his weapon aimed directly at Jack.

Just as Langston pulled the trigger, Monroe's shot rang out. The bullet struck Langston's arm, forcing him to drop his weapon with a howl of pain. The world seemed to slow as Langston staggered backward, clutching his bleeding arm, his face contorted in fury. Jack didn't waste a second. He sprinted toward the control console, pushing past the groaning soldiers who scrambled to regain their footing. The countdown timer on the screen flashed dangerously—three minutes remaining.

This was it. There was no turning back now. The fate of the world hung in the balance.

Chapter 12
The Final Countdown

The room erupted into chaos as gunfire rang out, the sharp, metallic sounds echoing off the walls of the control center. Jack's heart pounded in his chest, adrenaline coursing through his veins as he dove for cover behind a cluster of servers. His thoughts were a blur, only one thing clear in his mind: they couldn't let Langston activate the satellites. If the broadcast went live, it was all over. The world would fall under Olympus's control, and humanity's freedom would be gone forever.

Langston stood in the center of the room, his eyes burning with fury. "You think you can stop me?" he shouted, his voice filled with a mixture of disbelief and rage. "You're nothing but insects, trying to fight a force you can't even comprehend!"

Victor's voice rang out from behind a console, his voice steady even as gunfire whizzed past. "You're wrong, Langston! This ends now!"

Jack peeked over the top of the server rack, his eyes scanning the room for an opportunity. Monroe was already on the move, taking out one of Langston's soldiers with a precise shot to the head, her movements fluid and controlled. She was a force of nature, and Jack felt a surge of respect as he watched her expertly disarm another soldier, leaving him unconscious on the floor.

But Langston wasn't going down without a fight. He was a trained soldier, a ruthless strategist, and he had no intention of letting this mission fail. His eyes darted from one corner of the room to the other, calculating, always calculating.

In a blur of motion, Langston sprinted toward the control console, his weapon raised. The countdown timer on the screen flashed dangerously—three minutes remaining. He was almost there.

"No!" Jack shouted, his voice a raw mixture of panic and determination. He leapt from his hiding spot, charging toward Langston with everything he had.

Langston's smirk twisted into a vicious grin as he swung around, aiming his gun at Jack. "You think you can stop this, Jack? You're too late."

Time seemed to slow as Jack felt the weight of the moment crash down on him. The world around him narrowed to the barrel of Langston's gun and the fading sound of the countdown ticking away. Two minutes.

Monroe was quick, her instincts sharp. She moved faster than Jack could react, sliding into Langston's line of sight from the left and firing a single shot. The bullet hit Langston's arm, forcing him to drop his weapon with a howl of pain.

Jack took the opening without hesitation. He sprinted toward the control console, pushing past the groaning soldiers who scrambled to regain their footing. Langston staggered backward, clutching his bleeding arm, his face contorted in fury.

"You think this will stop me?" Langston snarled, his eyes burning with an unrelenting hatred. "This is bigger than you. Bigger than your pathetic little resistance. You can't stop it."

Monroe didn't hesitate. She aimed directly at Langston's chest, her voice cold and unwavering. "I'm not trying to stop you, Langston. I'm here to end this. Permanently."

With a sharp, quick shot, Monroe silenced Langston, the bullet piercing his heart before he could react. His body crumpled to the ground, the last vestiges of defiance fading from his eyes.

The room fell into silence, the weight of the moment hanging over them. The only sound was the relentless ticking of the countdown timer, now only one minute remaining.

"Victor!" Jack shouted, his voice hoarse. "We need to shut this down now!"

Victor was already at the central console, his hands flying across the controls. Sweat poured down his face as he worked with precision, trying to override the system, but the red lights flashing across the screen only made the situation more dire. The satellite feed had already been activated. The network was alive. The global system was preparing to broadcast.

Jack's stomach dropped. They were running out of time. Forty-five seconds.

"Come on, come on!" Victor muttered under his breath, his fingers flying over the keys in desperation. His face was etched with the weight of failure, but there was no way he was going to let Olympus win—not after everything they had been through.

Monroe stood at the door, watching for any reinforcements. Her eyes flicked to the countdown timer, her heart racing. They needed to disable the system now, or it would be too late. There was no other choice.

"We can't let it activate," Monroe said, her voice tinged with urgency. "This is it. We've fought too long for this."

Jack's mind raced. His pulse thudded in his temples, and a suffocating feeling settled in his chest. He couldn't afford to fail.

The future of humanity depended on their actions in these next moments.

Victor's hands paused over the console. He looked up at them both, his eyes heavy with the weight of years of resistance. "The satellite controls are linked to a self-repair protocol. Even if we destroy the servers here, the backup systems in orbit will kick in and take over unless we can hack the system from the outside."

Monroe gritted her teeth. "And how do we do that?"

"There's a relay system," Victor said, "just outside the facility. If I can manually access the uplink and destroy the relay, we can stop the satellites from sending the activation signal. It's a long shot, but it's the only way."

"Then let's go," Jack said, determination burning in his chest. He could feel the heat of the countdown rising, every second making it harder to breathe. They had no time to waste. "We don't have much left."

Victor nodded grimly. He grabbed a bag of tools from a storage compartment and started toward the exit. "Stay close. If we don't make it there before the countdown hits zero, this entire facility will go into lockdown, and the satellites will be live before we can stop them."

The three of them sprinted toward the exit, the distant hum of the facility growing louder as they approached the outside. The bitter wind bit at their skin as they emerged into the cold night. The snow had stopped falling, but the sky was still a blanket of dark clouds, the world around them eerily quiet.

But that silence was short-lived.

Suddenly, a barrage of gunfire erupted from the distance, cutting through the air like a vicious storm. The sharp cracks of weapons being discharged rattled their bones, and Jack instinctively ducked behind a cluster of nearby crates. They were surrounded. More of Langston's soldiers had arrived.

"They know we're here," Monroe growled, crouching behind cover. "We don't have much time!"

Victor didn't hesitate. He dove toward the nearest soldier, tackling him to the ground with the force of a freight train. Jack followed, drawing his weapon and firing in quick, precise bursts at the advancing troops. Each shot counted. They couldn't afford to miss.

Monroe moved with deadly precision, taking down one soldier after another. Her face was a mask of focus, her weapon never wavering from her target.

"We need to move!" Jack shouted, spotting the relay station in the distance, a small building tucked just outside the main facility. The relay tower's signal was pulsing like a beacon, but they had to destroy it to ensure Olympus's satellites wouldn't activate.

Victor gritted his teeth, his eyes narrowed with determination. "Cover me!"

Without waiting for a response, he sprinted toward the relay station, bullets whizzing past him as Jack and Monroe laid down cover fire. The soldiers were closing in, but they had no choice—they had to push forward.

"Go! Go! Go!" Monroe shouted, her voice ringing through the chaos.

Victor reached the relay station and quickly set to work, prying open the control panel. He was moving quickly but methodically, his hands shaking from the pressure of the situation. Jack and Monroe kept firing, holding the line as best they could, but the enemy was relentless. More soldiers were pouring in from the perimeter.

Thirty seconds.

Victor ripped out a cable from the panel, and sparks flew as he disconnected the power to the relay. For a moment, nothing happened, and Jack's heart sank. Had they failed?

But then, the satellite's signal cut off. The relay went dark. The countdown stopped.

For a moment, the world stood still. The relentless ticking of the timer ceased. The darkness surrounding them seemed to lift, and the weight of the mission hung in the air. The satellites would not activate. They had done it.

Victor stumbled back from the relay station, his face etched with exhaustion and relief. "It's done," he whispered. "We did it."

Monroe nodded, her breath heavy as she slumped against the side of the relay station. Her face was streaked with sweat, dirt, and blood, but the satisfaction in her eyes was unmistakable. "We stopped Olympus. We saved the world."

Jack couldn't speak. He was too overwhelmed, too exhausted to process everything. But as he stood there, his chest heaving, the sound of distant sirens started to echo through the cold mountain air. Their fight wasn't over.

Chapter 13
The Dawn of Freedom

The snow around Cedar Springs was eerily still, the chaos that had erupted moments before now giving way to a tense silence. The towering peaks of the mountains seemed to loom like silent witnesses, their jagged faces catching the last of the moonlight. Jack, Monroe, and Victor stood in the clearing, their weapons lowered but their minds still racing. They had done it. They had taken down Olympus—destroyed the satellite network and cut off the neural control that could have enslaved millions of people across the world.

But victory had come at a steep cost. The ground was littered with the bodies of the soldiers who had fought to protect Olympus. Some of them were dead, their bodies still warm, while others were wounded or unconscious. The grim reality of battle had set in. Even though their mission had succeeded, the consequences of their actions were far from over.

Jack wiped the sweat from his brow, his heart still pounding in his chest. Despite their success, there was no time to bask in the glow of victory. The battle for humanity's freedom wasn't over—not by a long shot. They had dismantled the heart of the project, but Olympus had far-reaching arms. There were still governments, corporations, and military forces across the globe that would fight to keep their control intact.

"We did it," Monroe said, her voice almost a whisper. She stood next to Jack, her eyes scanning the dark horizon as if searching for the next challenge. "But it doesn't feel like a win. Not yet."

Victor let out a sigh, his face drawn with exhaustion. "This is just the beginning, Monroe. We've taken down the central system, but Olympus is an idea. It's embedded in the fabric of society. The governments, the corporations—they'll find a way to rebuild it. We've made a dent, but the war is far from over."

Jack nodded grimly, his gaze falling to the bodies around them. They had won the battle, but they hadn't yet won the war. The world was still divided, still under the thumb of shadowy organizations and corrupt governments that operated in the dark. It wasn't just about taking down Olympus—it was about dismantling the systems of control that had been in place for so long.

"The question is," Jack said, his voice low, "what comes next? We've destroyed their ability to control the masses, but we've created a power vacuum. Someone else will try to fill it. And if we're not careful, we could end up with something even worse."

Victor glanced over at Jack, his face hardening with resolve. "That's why we need to act fast. We can't let this moment slip away. We need to keep the pressure on, expose the corruption at every level, and build a new system—a fairer one. One that doesn't rely on manipulation and control."

Monroe folded her arms, her expression thoughtful. "But who leads it? Who decides what's fair?"

"That's what we're going to find out," Victor replied. "The first step is making sure this technology never gets used again.

We need to make sure that Olympus—whatever form it may take—can't rebuild."

Jack looked at Victor, his determination clear. "And how do we do that?"

Victor's gaze was unwavering. "We gather every piece of intel we can find, make sure it's all exposed. We need to show the world what Olympus was, and we need to make sure that the people who tried to control it pay for their actions. If we don't, then it won't just be the military and the governments who try to use this power—it'll be the private corporations, the billionaires who see it as their ticket to unlimited power."

Jack clenched his fists, the weight of the world pressing down on him. "We've already seen what they're capable of. But if we can expose them—if we can show the truth—we might be able to take back control."

Monroe looked out at the distant mountains, her mind working as fast as her body had been in the heat of the battle. "I think we have a chance. But it's going to take more than just the three of us. We'll need allies—people from all walks of life, in all corners of the world. If we're going to make this stick, we need to ignite the revolution."

Victor nodded. "It won't be easy, but it's the only way."

Days passed in a blur as Jack, Monroe, and Victor worked tirelessly to cover their tracks. The world was still reeling from the sudden shutdown of the satellite network, the abrupt end to the global control systems that had governed people's thoughts and actions. The resistance had made their mark, but they had also left behind a trail of chaos. Every government, every institution that had been complicit in the rise of Olympus was now scrambling to restore order.

But the world was waking up.

Victor, Jack, and Monroe knew that they had to act quickly, before the powers that be could regroup and try to spin the narrative in their favor. They started by reaching out to the few allies they had left—those who had resisted Olympus from the beginning. These were the whistleblowers, the hackers, the journalists, and the underground movements that had been fighting back against the system long before Jack's team had ever known about Olympus.

The communications were sparse, encrypted, and often delayed, but they managed to put together a network—a patchwork of voices that would become the backbone of the new resistance. They were a ragtag group, but they were united in one common goal: to ensure that Olympus never rose again.

Jack's role was critical. He had been the one to bring the fight to Olympus, and now he had to help guide the resistance through the chaotic aftermath. He traveled across borders, speaking to leaders in the shadows—people who had long fought against corporate greed, government corruption, and the surveillance state. Some were wary of Jack and his team at first, unsure of their motives. But as the evidence of Olympus's reach grew clearer, more and more people joined the cause.

Monroe became a voice of reason in the resistance, pushing for a new world that didn't rely on the same corrupt structures that had allowed Olympus to thrive. Her sharp strategic mind, honed through years of military experience, was invaluable in organizing the resistance's efforts.

But it was Victor who became the face of the movement. His knowledge of Olympus and his connections within the intelligence community gave him the credibility needed to rally people to their cause. He had always been a soldier, a warrior, but now he was becoming a symbol of hope for those who had long been oppressed.

Together, they pushed forward, but the road was treacherous. Governments that had been compromised by Olympus fought back, attempting to discredit the movement and label them as terrorists. But they were no longer fighting with shadows and secrecy—they were fighting for the truth.

And as their efforts grew, so too did the resistance.

Months passed. The world was in turmoil, but it was a different kind of turmoil now. People were no longer living in fear of unseen control. They were waking up, questioning the very systems they had once believed in. There were protests in the streets of major cities across the globe—riots in some places, peaceful demonstrations in others. The people were demanding change, and for the first time in a long time, it seemed like the world was on the brink of something new.

In every corner of the globe, people were tearing down the old systems. Governments that had relied on surveillance and manipulation were falling. Corporate empires that had been built on exploitation and secrecy were crumbling. The global economy, once held together by the thin thread of control provided by Olympus, was in freefall.

But in the midst of the chaos, hope began to emerge.

Jack watched from a hidden location in the mountains as the news spread: the world was waking up. The resistance had gone viral. The information they had uncovered about Olympus, the secretive technologies, and the connections between the world's most powerful organizations was now being shared by millions. The truth was spreading faster than anyone could have imagined, and with it came the possibility of a new world—one where people would no longer be controlled by invisible forces.

"This is it," Monroe said as she sat beside Jack, watching the news feed. "We've ignited the fire. Now, we have to make sure it doesn't burn out."

Victor was at a table across the room, deep in conversation with a group of resistance leaders from around the world. "This won't be easy," he said, his voice filled with resolve. "We're up against decades of manipulation. But if we stay united, if we stay strong, we can rebuild."

Jack took a deep breath, looking out over the horizon as the first light of dawn began to break. The world had changed. They had changed it. And now, it was up to them—and to all those who had joined the cause—to rebuild.

The dawn of a new world had begun.

The fight for humanity's freedom was far from over, but for the first time in years, Jack, Monroe, and Victor saw a future full of possibility.

It was a world without Olympus. A world where humanity was free.

Chapter 14
The Last Stand

The world had changed. In the months following the dismantling of Olympus, society had shifted in ways that few could have imagined. Governments that once controlled their populations through surveillance and manipulation were beginning to crumble. People who had been shackled by fear and doubt were standing tall in the streets, demanding accountability, transparency, and a new way forward. It was a time of unrest, a time of hope, and yet, amidst the growing chaos, a quiet, sinister force lingered in the shadows, waiting for its moment to strike.

Jack, Monroe, and Victor stood in the heart of what had once been the Olympus control center—a place that now stood as a symbol of resistance. The walls, once lined with screens and surveillance equipment, were now covered in maps, blueprints, and charts. Resistance fighters from all corners of the globe had gathered here, united in their cause: to prevent the remnants of Olympus from rebuilding.

But beneath the optimism that filled the air, there was a growing unease. The job was far from over.

"We've come a long way," Monroe said, her voice carrying the weight of the battle they had fought. "But there's still more to do. Olympus might be gone, but its legacy isn't. There are still factions out there—corporations, military elites, politicians—all with their own agendas."

Jack nodded, his eyes fixed on the map in front of him. "We've exposed the truth, but the people who benefitted from Olympus's control are still out there, waiting for a chance to seize power again. We can't let that happen. We need to build something stronger—something permanent."

Victor stood by the window, watching the horizon as he thought over the growing network of resistance cells scattered across the world. "The problem is, there's no one central place to attack anymore. Olympus was a structure we could target. But now, it's a fractured system, and we've only put a crack in it. The battle has changed. We've lost the element of surprise."

Monroe turned toward him, her brow furrowed. "So what now? We've taken down their satellites. We've exposed their lies. The people are rising up, but we still don't have a clear target. We can't keep fighting this fight in the shadows forever."

Victor turned to face the group, his expression grim. "There's one last thing we need to do. One final piece of the puzzle."

Late into the night, Jack sat alone in the command center, reviewing the intelligence they had gathered over the past few months. There were hundreds of files, documents, and encrypted transmissions that had been uncovered from various Olympus facilities, but one thing stood out: a series of communications between key figures—high-ranking officials, corporate executives, and world leaders—all referencing something known only as Project Phoenix.

The files on Project Phoenix were scarce, but they suggested something far more dangerous than anything they had encountered so far. While Olympus may have been the public face of global control, Project Phoenix was something much deeper—something buried beneath layers of secrecy.

Jack had always known there was something off about their mission. Every time they seemed to land a blow against Olympus, they uncovered another piece of a much larger puzzle. He had hoped that taking down the satellite network and exposing the truth would signal the end of the struggle. But the more he uncovered, the more he realized that Project Phoenix was not just a continuation of Olympus—it was something far more insidious.

Monroe entered the room, breaking Jack from his thoughts. "You're up late. Found something?"

Jack gestured to the files in front of him. "I think we've only scratched the surface. These files reference something called Project Phoenix. From what I can gather, it's a global initiative designed to replace Olympus. But this time... it's not about controlling minds. It's about total domination through advanced biotechnology and nanotechnology."

Monroe's face darkened. "Biotechnology? What are they trying to do?"

"Upgrade humanity," Jack said slowly. "Implants, genetic modifications, neural enhancements... They're looking to create a new type of human being—one that's completely loyal and fully under their control. And they've already begun testing it in secret."

Victor's voice cut through the silence, as he stepped into the room. "You're saying this is worse than Olympus? This is about controlling people on a genetic level?"

Jack nodded, grimly. "Exactly. And from the looks of these files, it's already happening in some places—secret facilities all over the world. Project Phoenix is the real goal. Olympus was just a stepping stone."

Victor's fists clenched. "Then we need to stop it before it's too late."

Jack looked up at him, his eyes determined. "We can't let them complete Project Phoenix. If they do, it'll be the end of free will as we know it."

Monroe was silent for a moment before speaking again. "Where do we find these facilities? How do we even begin to shut something like that down?"

Jack met her gaze, his heart pounding. "We start with the source. The files point to a location—somewhere in the Arctic. That's where the research is being conducted, and we need to get there before it's too late."

Victor nodded. "Then we have no time to lose."

The plan was set in motion within days. The resistance had managed to secure a series of underground tunnels, which would lead them to the Arctic base where Project Phoenix was being developed. It was a place so remote, so well-guarded, that only a few knew of its existence. But Jack, Monroe, and Victor weren't going to let that stop them.

The journey was treacherous. The cold was unlike anything they had ever experienced. The biting winds cut through their clothes, and the snow seemed to fall in endless sheets, blurring their path. As they neared the facility, the landscape became increasingly desolate, a wasteland of ice and rock.

But the closer they got, the more they began to sense that something wasn't right. There was no sign of any military presence—no guards, no sentries, no security systems. It was as if the base had been abandoned.

"Something's wrong," Monroe said, her voice tinged with suspicion. "This is too quiet."

Jack's heart raced. He'd known it wouldn't be easy, but this felt... off. "Stay alert. We don't know what we're walking into."

Victor unslung his rifle, his face set with determination. "Let's move. We're almost there."

As they made their way closer to the base, they noticed something even more unsettling: large, metallic structures rising from the ground, glowing faintly in the darkness. These weren't just research buildings—they were labs, testing facilities, and something else... something far darker.

Jack's stomach dropped as he took in the sight. "This is it. This is Project Phoenix."

But just as they were about to breach the outer perimeter of the base, the ground beneath them trembled. A loud, deep rumble echoed through the frozen landscape, followed by a series of blinding lights. The sky above them seemed to light up in an unnatural blaze, casting long shadows across the ice.

"What the hell is that?" Monroe demanded, looking up in confusion and fear.

Jack barely had time to react when a voice crackled through their communication channels, a voice they thought they'd never hear again.

"It's too late, Jack," Langston's voice echoed, cold and menacing. "Project Phoenix has already begun. And you've just walked into my trap."

The ground shook again, this time with enough force to knock them off their feet. Jack scrambled to his feet, his mind racing. The trap had already been set. They were too late.

"No," Jack muttered, his heart sinking. "No..."

The lights above flickered and went out. In the dark, something moved—something massive, emerging from the shadows. It was a mechanical monstrosity, a hybrid of technology and flesh, its eyes glowing with an eerie, unnatural light.

And then, in the distance, the sound of hundreds of others, just like it, coming to life.

Jack's blood ran cold as the realization hit him.

Project Phoenix wasn't just about controlling people. It was about creating an army—an army of genetically modified super soldiers, each one connected to a vast, unyielding system that controlled their every move.

This was no longer just a battle for freedom. It was a fight for survival.

As the monstrous figure loomed closer, Jack knew their struggle was far from over. In fact, it had just begun. What they had uncovered wasn't just a weapon—it was the dawn of a new, terrifying era.

And Jack, Monroe, and Victor were at the center of it.

"Get ready," Jack whispered, his voice barely audible over the sound of approaching footsteps. "This is just the beginning."

And then, everything went black.

TO BE CONTINUED...